W9-DBA-489

A Single Moment—Captured Forever—Before He Returned to the Alamo . . .

The slow, sweet smile that Lucy had seen every night in her dreams adorned Jesse Lee's face.

But then he was instantly serious. There was no resisting him. Dark circles gave his blue eyes the depth of black sapphires. . . .

"Lucy, this battle is making things happen so quick. I know you're brave enough for me to tell you—I don't know if we're going to make it out there. If anything happens to me, I want to have the memory of your sweet kiss on my lips."

Lucy didn't allow herself to think. She wanted to kiss Jesse Lee, wanted to have the memory of that kiss as much as he did.

She bent toward him. He was too weary to hold her in his arms. Their lips touched, as light as feathers, as soft as flowers. That's all there was, and afterward Lucy took a deep breath. She was trembling.

"I know," Jesse Lee took her hand, brought it to his lips, "I know. I love you, Lucy. . . ."

DAWN OF LOVE HISTORICAL ROMANCES for you to enjoy

#1 RECKLESS HEART
     by Dee Austin
#2 WILD PRAIRIE SKY
     by Cheri Michaels
#3 SAVAGE SPIRIT
     by Meg Cameron
#4 FEARLESS LOVE
     by Stephanie Andrews

Available from ARCHWAY paperbacks

FEARLESS LOVE

Stephanie Andrews

AN ARCHWAY PAPERBACK
Published by POCKET BOOKS • NEW YORK

AN ARCHWAY PAPERBACK *Original*

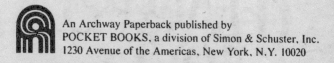

An Archway Paperback published by
POCKET BOOKS, a division of Simon & Schuster, Inc.
1230 Avenue of the Americas, New York, N.Y. 10020

ISBN: 0-671-55158-2

First Archway Paperback printing August, 1985

10 9 8 7 6 5 4 3 2 1

AN ARCHWAY PAPERBACK and colophon are registered trademarks of Simon & Schuster, Inc.

DAWN OF LOVE is a registered trademark of Bruck Communications, Inc.

Printed in the U.S.A.

IL 7+

FEARLESS LOVE

Chapter 1

"LUCY! HEY, LUCY!—"

Lucy Bonner heard her brother call from clear across the inner courtyard of Fort Alamo. She turned and saw Carlos struggling to keep a giant pot of hot basting sauce from tipping over.

Poor Carlos, Lucy thought. It was hard enough being on the small side for a boy. But surrounded now by the rough-and-tumble men who had come to help the Texans fight for their independence from Mexico, Carlos had to be even more aware of his diminutive size. She ran quickly across the flat, packed dirt of the fort to his side. "Carlos—here, I'll take one handle and you take the other."

For a minute the cauldron swayed dangerously between them. Then Lucy and Carlos steadied the heavy cast-iron pot, carrying it to the pit where a steer was slowly barbecuing over a mesquite fire.

"Just in time," their cook Ramiro said, and he dipped a clean broom into the sauce to baste the roasting meat. His white teeth gleamed as he smiled beneath his dark mustache. "We show the *norteños* how we eat *vaquero* style in Texas, *correcto?*"

"*Correcto,*" Lucy said, offering Ramiro the half-shy, half-seductive smile of a properly brought-up *señorita*.

Carlos's grin matched Ramiro's. "Not so correct," he said. "Ma and some of the other ladies are having fits at the idea of standing around, eating out in the open. They say Davy Crockett and those other men from Tennessee are going to think Texans don't have right good manners."

Lucy pushed a wave of blue-black hair off her forehead and stole a peek at the group of men standing huddled off in a corner of the fort. Big-boned they were, the men from Tennessee, as if living in the backwoods had somehow made them grow beefy, while Texans tended to be more angular and lean. One of the younger men glanced in her direction. Lucy quickly cast her brown eyes down—but not soon enough to avert the sudden and disturbing thrill that rippled through her. Yes, the Texans were lucky to have the Tennesseans—Davy Crockett and his men— on their side. The Mexicans would think twice before they made a promise to Texas and then took it back!

Out of the corner of her eye, Lucy caught the young man from Tennessee still staring at her. Her beige cheeks felt warm in the night air. *I ought to be scan-*

dalized at such boldness, she told herself. But somehow she wasn't.

"Ma doesn't have to worry," she said to Ramiro as she caught her silky hair back in a scarlet ribbon. "I guess any Texan can match a backwoodsman from Tennessee when it comes to manners."

"*Seguro*," was Ramiro's opinion, and he stepped back to survey his handiwork. "Please tell Señora Bonner that I will need more sauce. Also, that I am too busy to prepare the rest of the dinner."

His words were apologetic, but Lucy caught a glimpse of Ramiro's satisfaction. The ladies of San Antonio would have to do their own cooking. He was preparing a meal for the men from Tennessee, as well as the other people who crowded the Alamo. Soon Ramiro wouldn't be cooking for them at all. Like the other men who usually cooked for the big ranches, he would be busy getting ready to defend the Alamo. Looking around, Lucy saw that, instead of cleaning pots, the ranch cooks were cleaning guns like all the other men.

"The idea!" Estrella Bonner said when Lucy gave her mother the message.

"Never mind, *querida*," William Bonner said to his wife, putting his arm about her tiny waist. "It's the least we can do. The twelve men from Tennessee are volunteers. They didn't have to come."

Estrella Bonner was shocked. "But—but eating out of doors?"

"It'll be fine, Ma," Lucy said, glancing again at the

3

men from Tennessee. "We'll pretend we're *vaqueros* out on roundup. And we're lucky—here it is February and it's not real cold."

"But we're not cowboys," her mother said, using the English word. "And these men who have come to the Alamo to help—we should serve them properly."

"There are too many of us to eat fancy," William Bonner said. "Around a hundred and fifty men, not to mention the woman and kids. Besides, we don't have time to worry about being proper just now."

Estrella looked at her husband with fear. "Are we in danger, William? I thought you said everything would be all right."

"Everything *will* be all right," William Bonner said, and he hugged his wife to him.

Over his wife's shoulder, he glanced at his daughter. She was delicate-boned and full of her mother's fragile beauty, but with a hidden core of his own flinty Virginia strength. It was there, beneath the carefully taught manners, just waiting to come out.

Lucy caught her father's glance. "Come on, Ma," she said gently. "I'll help you and the other ladies cook the beans and rice. Then we'll carry the food outside. You'll see, it'll be all right."

Estrella Bonner tried to smile as she and Lucy draped large white aprons over their full-skirted muslin dresses and helped with the cooking. William Bonner watched with adoring eyes as his wife and daughter, like two dark-haired, bright-eyed angels, carried

4

steaming earthenware casseroles brimming with food out to the courtyard.

The ranch hands had stopped cleaning their guns long enough to set up makeshift trestle tables, where Ramiro was now slicing meat and piling it especially high on the plates of the men who had followed Davy Crockett from Tennessee to Texas.

"More beans?" Lucy asked. It was strange to be a serving girl to strangers, and she was having trouble with the hot earthenware casserole that she was carrying from man to man. She could feel the heat through the cloth holders. "Help yourself, please."

The courtyard was lit with flaring torches, and she had to concentrate to keep from dropping the dish. Even so, she couldn't help stealing shy glances at the men who dipped the ladle into the bean pot.

"You better let me give you a hand with that," she heard someone say. "That's much too heavy for a little thang like you."

Thang. It was his pronunciation that caused her sudden smile. "I'm not so little," she began, and then she saw that it was him—the young man from Tennessee who had stared at her so boldly. The pot tipped over, and before she could straighten it his dusty boots were spattered with hot beans.

She stared up at him, too startled to say she was sorry. Now she saw what the flickering torchlight had concealed. He was the best-looking boy she had ever seen—so good-looking that it took her breath away. And tall! Most of the boys she knew in Texas were tall, and she was no little thing herself, even though he had called her that. But he was so tall that if she had leaned forward, her head could have rested against his chest, no higher than his heart. She thought of laying her cheek there and was shocked at herself.

"I—I'm sorry," Lucy stammered, glad that the boy from Tennessee couldn't read her thoughts.

There was a moment of silence when Lucy could almost feel the stranger's thoughts settling on her. Then he spoke, his words filled with wild twinges of the backwoods. Lucy's heart beat a shade faster in rhythm with them. "No need to be sorry," he said, smiling. "Here—you hold onto my plate, and I'll just take that big old pot from you." Then the tall stranger carried the pot to a nearby table.

She watched him turn back toward her, and she began to fear that her voice would give away the strange excitement she felt. Oh, she could chatter as easily as a bird to her family, but that was to her family. Strange boys, her mother had taught her, were to be approached with downcast eyes and great modesty. And not only was this boy a stranger, but his hair—the color of pale golden honey—and his eyes—the color of a deep blue sky—made him the best-looking stranger she had ever seen. Put that all together, and she was bound to act the fool.

He smiled, and the smile made him look even better. It wasn't fair. A chipped tooth would have made her feel a lot more comfortable.

"Jesse Lee Powell, ma'am. Come from Tennessee with old Davy there."

"I—I know," Lucy managed to say, her beige cheeks showing spots of rose.

He waited, and she tried to say her name, but the words suddenly stuck in her throat. *Lucy Bonner, I'm Lucy Bonner.* She'd only said that about a million times. Why couldn't she say it now?

He tried to make it easier for her to speak. "You work for one of the ranchers around here?"

That made her smile, and she felt a little easier. She could imagine her mother's reaction if she heard that Lucy was taken for somebody's cook. "Not exactly," she said. "I'm Lucy Bonner."

"Well, Miss Lucy, I'm sure pleased to meet you."

He didn't know who she was, Lucy realized. The Bonner name meant nothing to him, and why should it? For all she knew, Jesse Lee Powell's family could own the biggest ranch, or farm, or whatever they had in Tennessee.

"And—and I'm pleased to meet you, Mr. Powell," Lucy said. "It was fine of you to come from Tennessee to help people you don't even know."

"My name's Jesse Lee. You call me Mr. Powell and I figure you're talking to my pa. I don't know if it was so all-fired fine. I just followed old Davy, and he'll do anything for a scrap."

The blond man's smile came down at her from about a million miles away, and Lucy couldn't help smiling

7

back. Then, with his body leaning just close enough to hers to ease her next to him, they began to stroll the length of Fort Alamo's courtyard.

"There's a lot riding on what's going to happen here," Jesse Lee said. "After all, if Mexico can promise Texas statehood and then go back on their deal, people in the southwest territories are going to start worrying about their borders."

Lucy simply shook her head, content to say nothing and listen to his twangy masculine voice. Jesse Lee didn't seem to mind doing the talking.

"Yup, Santy Anny is going to outsmart himself this time around, I'll wager. With men like old Davy here, we're bound to fend off the Mexican Army. I know we can."

"Of course we can!" Lucy said, so enthusiastically she surprised herself.

Soon they came to a group of people gathered around the two commanders of the Alamo, Jim Bowie and William Barrett Travis. Next to them was a man wearing a fringed buckskin shirt and a cap festooned with a raccoon's tail. "That's him," Jesse Lee whispered. "That's old Davy himself."

"We want to say thanks," big Jim Bowie was saying, "to Davy Crockett and to everyone who came with him—"

"No need for that," Davy Crockett drawled. "We heard you were having trouble with old Santy Anny and we allowed as how we might help. We like a good fight. Here it is eighteen hundred and thirty-six, and I haven't had a good fight since eighteen-twelve."

The men cheered and the women applauded, and as the two groups mingled another man from Tennessee came up to Jesse Lee and looked admiringly at Lucy.

"Doesn't take you no time at all, does it, Jesse Lee? You always find the prettiest girl before the rest of us even get a chance to look around."

"I'm just lucky," Jesse Lee said, smiling. "Sometimes pretty girls just come my way . . . spilling beans."

Lucy caught the other man's appraising glance and, sensing danger, took a step closer to Jesse Lee. "Look a' that!" the other man said. "Pretty as a dark red rose. Part Mex, I bet. The best kind—real warm blood runs in their veins, from what I hear." Now Lucy felt her face flame.

Jesse Lee stepped forward. His voice was low, but there was a note of menace in it. "Watch your mouth, Harper," he said to the other man. "This here's a lady. Can't you tell that?"

"Lady!" the man said, laughing and looking at Lucy's once white apron, now food-spattered, and at her long black hair which had come loose from its red ribbon. "Lady—"

He didn't have a chance to say another word before Jesse Lee sent him sprawling in the dust. There might have been more words between the two men, but Lucy didn't wait to hear them. She ran across the courtyard and stood close to her father and their friends from San Antonio.

Her father was listening to the conversation between Colonel Travis and Davy Crockett, so he didn't notice that Lucy was upset.

"What's the matter, *mi novia?*" Captain Juan Seguin, who was standing close by, asked softly. "What has happened to upset my best girl?"

Lucy shook her head. She didn't want to tell Juan what had sent her running across the courtyard. Somehow she felt responsible. If she had been demure and unapproachable, this might not have happened. "Beauty is a rose," her mother had often warned her. "A flower with thorns in it." Lucy smiled silently at Juan Seguin. The Bonners and the Seguins had been friends for years, and as a little girl she had had the most awful crush on the darkly handsome Juan. He had been kind and had never made fun of her, not even when she told him, when she was ten and he was twenty, that she wanted to be his sweetheart, his *novia*.

Lucy had outgrown her childish crush, but Juan never forgot the little girl who had told him how much she loved him. His concern for her now was evident. "Lucy," he asked again. "Lucy?"

"Nothing," she whispered, her throat tight. "It's nothing, Juan."

It would have ended there if Jesse Lee hadn't come looking for her. He put his hand on her shoulder as he came up behind her and said, "Real sorry about that, Miss Lucy. That Harper's a right fool."

Juan's voice was sharp. "What happened, Lucy?" he asked, glaring at Jesse Lee Powell.

Lucy wanted to sink into the ground. All this fuss! She didn't want to tell Juan how upset she had been by the way that man Harper had looked at and spoken to her. She knew how protective Juan felt toward her. But before she could stop him, Jesse Lee was explaining what had occurred to the tall captain of the Texas forces.

"A misunderstanding," he tried to reassure Juan. "And I'm real sorry if Miss Lucy was offended—"

"Offended?" Juan bristled.

William Bonner turned. "Has someone offended Lucy?" he asked. "Lucy? What happened?"

"Nothing," Lucy said, wishing all these men would stop fussing over her.

But now both Juan and her father had turned on Jesse Lee Powell.

"What happened?"

"What did you do to Lucy?"

"Oh, please—" Lucy said. She was in the center, surrounded by the three men.

"I said I was sorry," Jesse Lee said to Juan. "And I don't see that it's your concern—"

"Anything that happens to Lucy is my concern," Juan said angrily.

"And I'm Lucy's father." William Bonner's eyes contained a threat.

Lucy saw it all happening again—a repetition of what had gone on a few minutes before.

Her father and Juan glared at Jesse Lee, who glared right back. There were two of them against him, but Lucy had seen the way Jesse Lee moved. He was as fast as a cougar, and she pictured both her father and Juan sprawling in the dust with all their friends from San Antonio ringed curiously about them.

It was Jesse Lee and Davy Crockett who saved the day.

Jesse Lee did it by laughing. He threw his head back and laughed—a hearty, open laugh—and when he looked at Lucy his eyes sparkled with admiration. "Nothing like a pretty girl to get men a-fighting, and I guess you're the prettiest girl hereabouts, so you're sure worth a fight. Except—except that I'm not really sure what we'd be fighting about."

Davy Crockett had moved through the crowd, and now he stood beside his Tennessee sharpshooter. "I don't know you, sir," he said to William Bonner, "but I've known this big old boy here for most all of his nineteen years, and I don't believe he'd do anything to offend this pretty little lady." He smiled at Lucy and then at her father. "Your daughter, is she?"

William Bonner nodded and looked at Lucy again. "Lucy?" he asked.

"Pa," she said. "It was nothing." Lucy felt a surge of admiration for the way Jesse Lee had handled the situation. She stole a glance in his direction and saw that his deep blue eyes still held the twinkle of his laugh. She just wished she had the words to explain that it was Jesse Lee who had defended her against that insulting man, Harper. But she couldn't go into a long explanation—not in front of all those people. "Pa," she said again. "Please."

"Well," William Bonner said, nodding to Juan Seguin, who still looked angry. "I guess it's all right." With one more long, meaningful look at Jesse Lee, he walked off to look for his wife.

Davy Crockett clapped his arm around Jesse Lee's shoulders, and the two men moved off.

"Save the fighting for Santy Anny," Lucy heard him say to Jesse Lee. "That's what we come for."

Lucy sighed as she saw Jesse Lee Powell move away without so much as a backward glance. She'd never see him again, that was for sure, and why should she care? They had met and spoken for only a few minutes. It didn't mean anything. *Except that I do care,* Lucy admitted to herself wonderingly. *I do care!*

It was sharp-eyed Juan Seguin who saw something in Lucy's face—something her father hadn't noticed. "Plenty of good men right here in San Antonio, Lucy," Juan said sharply. "No need getting interested in some stranger."

"I'm not interested in anybody," Lucy said, sudden sharpness edging her voice. "Goodness, I guess we all have other things to think about besides—besides—"

"Besides love," Juan said softly, and his liquid

13

brown eyes seemed to be looking at her in a new way. "You're grown up, Lucy. It's been a long time since you said you wanted to be my *novia*."

Lucy felt herself blush to the roots of her hair. "I was just a baby when I said that, Juan. You didn't take me seriously."

"No," Juan said lightly. "But perhaps I should have."

Lucy shook her head. It was so strange the way things happened. Just six years ago she would have died with happiness if Juan Seguin had said those words to her, but now she looked away from him, trying to spot the tall, broad-shouldered Jesse Lee Powell.

"He's over there," Juan said, understanding Lucy's searching look too well. "With Jim Bowie and Will Travis. Go ahead, Lucy. Don't let me stop you."

"I don't know what you mean," Lucy said. "I was looking for my mother."

"She's close by." Juan pointed, and his white teeth flashed in a smile. "If that's who you want to see."

Lucy had no more words for Juan. They had been friends for so long that perhaps he had the right to tease her. Even so, she felt as transparent as a drop of dew.

She turned and hurried to where her mother and father stood with their rancher neighbors, the Shumanns.

Chapter 2

"I'M LEAVING TOMORROW," JOHANN SHUMANN WAS saying. "Me and my family. We're heading back to the ranch with the first morning light. And you'd be wise to come with me, Bonner, you and your whole family."

Lucy's father shook his head. "I'd feel as though I was deserting if I did that," he said. "Davy Crockett and some good men came to stand beside us. I don't see letting them face Santa Anna alone."

Johann Shumann shrugged. "It's not my battle. I came here from Pennsylvania to ranch, and I don't reckon it matters to me what government we have as long as they leave me alone and let me do my ranching."

Lucy could see that her father was doing his best to

keep his temper. "Each man has got to do what he thinks is right," he said.

Estrella Bonner held on tightly to her husband's arm. She looked at Johann Shumann. "You said battle," she said. "Do you think there's going to be a battle, Mr. Shumann?"

Lucy saw her father's warning look, and she heard Mr. Shumann answer, "Probably not, ma'am. Probably Santa Anna and the Mexicans are bluffing, but I just figure it'll be safer back at the ranch. Bonner, why don't you send your family back with me if you're so all-fired determined to stay here?"

"A good idea," William Bonner said. He turned to his wife. "All this fuss'll be over in a few days, Estrella. You and Lucy and Carlos can wait for me at the ranch."

"No." Estrella Bonner's large dark eyes seemed to become even larger and darker. "I won't leave you, William."

"It's all right, *querida*," William Bonner said, soothing his wife. "It's all right." He placed one large hand over his wife's little graceful one, and Lucy was struck by the contrast of his sun-bronzed skin against her mother's exotic dark tones. Her mother's gold wedding band caught the lights of a hundred campfires, and suddenly Lucy envied them their bond, their love. "We're staying together," William Bonner told the Shumanns. And Lucy believed she was the only one to hear him say, "For the time being, anyway."

"I better help the ladies clear up," Lucy said.

"I'll go with you," her mother said.

"You stay here," William Bonner told his wife, still holding her close to him. "You've done enough for one day, Estrella. Go ahead, Lucy. You explain that your ma's tired."

"I'll go with you, Lucy," Dirk Shumann said.

Lucy wished she could tell him not to bother. There was nothing about short and stocky Dirk Shumann that she liked. She had heard somewhere that men who were on the heavy side were jolly and full of fun, but that certainly wasn't true about Dirk Shumann.

The Bonners and the Shumanns were neighboring ranchers, and Carlos and Lucy had been told to be friendly to Dirk, but both of them found it hard to be friendly with the serious and brooding young man who always seemed to be angling for something.

"We're just cleaning up," Lucy said as Dirk walked closely beside her across the courtyard of the mission-turned-fort. "Nothing you can do to help."

"I want to talk to you, Lucy," Dirk persisted. "This seems as good a chance as any."

Lucy sighed. Dirk had hinted at his intentions more than once, and now he came right out and told her what he had on his mind. Lucy only half listened—she was so completely uninterested in anything that Dirk had to say.

". . . and in time, the Bonner and Shumann ranches could be one of the biggest—one of the finest—ranches in the whole territory. . . ."

What was he saying? Even as she walked across the dirty courtyard, Lucy had been looking for the tall, slim figure of Jesse Lee Powell. She hadn't been paying attention to Dirk, and the whole time she was looking for Jesse Lee, Dirk Shumann had been proposing marriage to her!

"The idea, Dirk!" Lucy burst out, her dislike of him making her forget her good manners. "Whatever made you think that I'd be interested in marrying you?"

Dirk stopped talking. He stopped walking. He acted like a man who had been shot.

Oh, no, Lucy thought. *Whatever made me talk to him like that?* "I'm—I'm sorry, Dirk" Lucy stammered. "I—I didn't mean it quite that way. I—I mean we've always been friends—nothing more. Of course—I'm very, very honored—"

"You sure sound like you're honored," Dirk said bitterly.

"I was just so—so surprised, that's all," Lucy said. "Thank you, Dirk, but it wouldn't work out. You see," she said, afraid she was going to hurt him again, "I don't love you."

"Love? What has love got to do with it? We get along, don't we? Love'll come later, but this would be the best way to make sure that our ranches—"

"Oh, ranches be blamed!" Lucy practically shouted. "I'm not going to marry anybody because of a ranch."

"Well, I never thought to hear you talk like that." Dirk was genuinely shocked. Quiet, shy Lucy, using a word like *blamed!* That was almost as bad as using a word like *blasted*—and coming from a girl, too! He wished they had some Pennsylvania-Dutch neighbors near their ranch. No Amish girl would use a word like *blamed.* But then, Lucy's mother was of Mexican and Spanish descent—that probably accounted for it. He looked furtively at Lucy. She was a beauty—her clear, camellia petal-like skin and her blue-black hair always took his breath away—but that didn't excuse her crude, unwomanly behavior.

Still, it was the sight of her that made him say, "I reckon you're not yourself, Lucy, what with this worry about Santa Anna and all. We'll talk about this another time."

Never, Lucy wanted to say. *We'll never talk about this again.* But she decided she had said enough for one day.

"All right, Dirk. But I have to go now. There's a lot of clearing up to be done."

Dirk looked after Lucy as she walked toward the large pit where the barbecue fire still burned, and he saw the tall young man who came from the shadows to walk beside her. He felt the urge to follow them but quickly curbed it when he took a look at the big Tennessee man standing at Lucy's side. There would be lots of time to talk to Lucy. Dirk shrugged his shoulders and turned away.

"You break hearts right and left, don't you, Miss Lucy?" It was Jesse Lee Powell striding beside her, and Lucy could tell that he had heard everything—or almost everything—of the conversation she had had with Dirk Shumann.

"Mr. Powell—"

"Jesse Lee."

"You've been listening."

"Sure," he said, and he didn't seem one bit bothered by the accusing note in her voice. "My pa told me a man don't learn nothing if he don't listen."

Lucy laughed. She couldn't help it. Jesse Lee was so different from serious, sour Dirk. She had never in her whole life flirted with a boy, and she didn't think she knew how, but suddenly she wanted to flirt with Jesse Lee Powell.

"And my pa told me that if you listen in on conversations," she said, "you're liable to overhear some bad things about yourself."

"I'm not worried," Jesse Lee said. "You don't know me well enough to say anything bad about me—not yet, anyway."

"And if I did know you well enough? What would I say then?" Lucy asked.

"Nothing *too* terrible," Jesse Lee said. "I'm pretty tame for someone from Tennessee. Besides, I don't have as many girls crying into their pillows as you have boys marching around wondering what they did to make you say, 'Ranches be blamed.' "

"You did hear!"

"Sure I did," Jesse Lee said calmly. "Learned something about you, too."

"What could you have learned about me?"

"Learned that you're not the kind of girl who'd marry a man just because he's got a big ranch located right next to her pa's spread." Jesse Lee threw his head back and laughed. "Imagine me taking you for the hired help! That's one on me, all right."

"Does that matter?" Lucy asked, wishing that she didn't sound so all-fired serious.

But Jesse Lee answered her just as seriously. "Doesn't matter none to me," he told her. "Nothing mattered after I saw you, Lucy girl. I never felt this way before. I saw you, and I knew why it was I came to Texas. It wasn't to fight old Santy Anny after all."

Jesse Lee's words sent shivers through Lucy. The two of them stood close to each other, their faces illuminated by flickering firelight and the moon of a brilliant Texas night.

"This—this can't be," she said. "We just met a little while ago."

"Yep," Jesse Lee said. "I know that, but I also know that sometimes it happens that way. It happened that way to my folks. They met one night at a hoedown, and they both knew that was it for the two of them. Pa said he never looked at another girl after that, and Ma loved only him until the day she died. And if our preacher back home is right, she loves him still."

Lucy was somehow jarred out of the happiness of the moment by what Jesse Lee had said about his mother. "When did your mother die?" she asked.

"Two years ago," Jesse Lee said. "Made me know

then that time moves awful fast. Wish I had the time to court you proper, Lucy, but I came to Texas to fight, not make love, and none of us knows what tomorrow's going to bring. That's why I figured to speak my piece tonight."

Lucy shivered. "You do think there's going to be a fight, Jesse Lee?"

Jesse Lee hesitated. "Sure looks like, but don't you worry none. Like I said before, I reckon we can take care of any trouble the Mexicans care to send."

Lucy believed him. With men like Jesse Lee and her father at the Alamo, the San Antonians would be safe. Besides, they had beaten back a Mexican army just two short months before, and there was no reason they couldn't do it again.

Lucy looked up trustingly at Jesse Lee, and when he gently drew her close to him in the circle of his strong arms, she went willingly. He held her for a minute, and then he bent his head. Their lips were barely touching when they heard the raucous laughter from the shadows behind them.

"Don't waste no time, do you, Jesse Lee?" It was the man Jesse had called Harper. 'It works every time, don't it, boy? 'There may be a battle tomorrow, honey, so we best make hay tonight!' I guess I seen you pull that old chestnut maybe a dozen times by now."

"Jesse Lee!" Lucy pulled herself free from the warmth of his arms.

"Harper, you fool," Jesse Lee shouted angrily. "This is nothing like those other times—"

"Oh no," Lucy wailed. Jesse Lee hadn't even bothered to deny those other times. He was just trying to make her believe that this time was different.

What a fool she was, and she had made herself look no account in everyone's eyes. Lucy was sure that everyone—just everyone—had seen her in Jesse Lee Powell's arms. She knew what they all must think of her. She, who had always been too shy even to flirt with a man, had shamed herself and shamed her entire family in front of everyone in San Antonio! Lucy fled into the mission building, looking for someplace to hide until she could bring her emotions under control.

But there weren't many places to hide in the crowded building. The rooms of the mission had been converted into a makeshift fort, and bedding and belongings were heaped all along the walls. Trestle tables were piled high with plates and food, and pots and pans were all mixed in with mattresses, blankets, and clothing. One hundred and fifty men as well as some women and children had piled into the Alamo, and they had brought many of their belongings with them. Lucy couldn't find a corner where she could sit and cry in peace.

"Guess that buckskinned wildman doesn't look so good anymore, does he, Lucy?" It was the jeering voice of Dirk Shumann.

Lucy backed away from him.

"Oh, I saw you all right—hugging and kissing with a man you never saw before in your whole life. And me wanting to make you my wife!"

As upset as she was about Jesse Lee Powell, Lucy couldn't let Dirk Shumann talk to her like that. There were times when a body just had to speak out, Lucy decided, and this surely was one of them. Shaking with emotion and anger, Lucy whirled on him. Back home she would have kept it in, but then again, back home a lot of things wouldn't be happening. Suddenly Lucy found the words to tell Dirk just what she thought of him.

"You have no right spying on me, Dirk Shumann, especially when I told you clear as day that I wouldn't marry you. And anyway, there was just one little hug, and no kissing, and bother—I don't know why I'm talking to you about this anyway! It's none of your blamed business!"

Lucy turned, longing to move far away from Dirk. But where? Texans were used to a lot of space—they took it for granted—and now here they were, all so crowded together they barely had room to breathe!

And if being crowded by Dirk Shumann wasn't bad enough, Jesse Lee came striding through the crowded rooms, looking for Lucy. "You've got to let me explain," he said, shouldering his way past Dirk.

Lucy surprised herself again. "I don't want to talk to you," she told him, not bothering to keep her emotions in check. Then she stepped back, her skirts whirling about her, her dark eyes flashing with anger.

"Tell him, Lucy," Dirk said with a mean little laugh. "Even though you're telling him too late."

"And I don't want to talk to you either, Dirk Shumann—not ever again." And then, much to her own dismay, Lucy burst into tears. "You're horrible—both of you!"

It was Juan Seguin who saved Lucy from any more trouble with the two men. Lucy didn't know how much he had seen or heard of what had happened between the three of them, but he spoke in a strong, quiet voice that made it clear he meant what he said. "Leave Lucy alone, both of you. Dirk, you're to stop plaguing her. And you," he said, turning to Jesse Lee Powell, "if you go on this way, you may find yourself fighting this Mexican before you even catch sight of Santa Anna and his army."

"Juan," Lucy said, trembling. "Please take me outside. I don't want Ma and Pa to know about all this."

"Of course." Juan offered Lucy his arm, and this courtly gesture made Lucy stop crying. Her head went up and her back straightened. Walking like a princess, she stepped past Dirk and Jesse Lee as though they didn't exist.

Chapter 3

LUCY SPENT A RESTLESS NIGHT IN ONE TINY CORNER of a stone-walled room in the mission. She and her mother shared one lumpy mattress while her father and Carlos shared another. Everyone slept in their clothes, and in the morning the two Bonner women did their best to adjust their dresses and smooth their hair.

"If only I could take a bath," Estrella Bonner said, "put on a fresh dress—"

"Perhaps you should go back to the ranch," William Bonner said. "You'd be more comfortable there—you and the children."

"We will stay with you," she told him. The fragility of Estrella Bonner's beauty was eclipsed by her determination to stay at her husband's side. "That is what I want, and I'm sure that is what Carlos and Lucy want, too."

"Of course," Lucy said.

"And if there's going to be any fighting," Carlos said, "I want to stand right next to you, Pa."

William Bonner laughed and ruffled his son's sandy brown hair. "What a family! If General Santa Anna knew that he had the Bonners to face, I reckon he'd turn tail and run right back to where he came from."

William Bonner gathered his family close to him, and when Lucy returned his hug she decided that she would never, ever leave her family. She didn't want to hear anything more about love and marriage. She'd live and die with her parents, she thought, convinced that the best thing to be in the whole world was an old maid!

Lucy and Carlos went to the well in the courtyard, where they lined up with the others for pitchers of water. The four Bonners used one pitcherful to wash their faces and hands, and the other pitcherful went into an old tin coffee pot. The dirty courtyard of the Alamo had many small fires going every morning as the San Antonians prepared pot after pot of inky black coffee.

"We can hold the Alamo forever," was Jim Bowie's comment as he moved from one fire to another, accepting and drinking endless cups of coffee. "We got water and we got coffee—and a Texan can live on strong coffee forever."

But the cheerful mood of the Alamo was subdued when some of the men began readying wagons for their families to leave the Alamo.

"I'll leave you the good mattress," Lucy heard one woman say to her husband, "and all the blankets . . ."

"Here's a coffee pot," she heard another say, "and the iron skillet . . ."

"I'm not going in for any fancy cooking," her husband answered with a laugh. "You just take the skillet and start frying up some chicken for me when I get home."

"Estrella, maybe," William Bonner said to his wife, "maybe—"

"No," Estrella Bonner replied. "Absolutely not, William."

But despite Estrella Bonner's resolve, William Bonner was determined that his family would leave after a scout on a lathered pinto horse rode into the Alamo. The tall wooden doors had been swung open so that the wagons could leave the fort, but before they could leave the scout galloped in.

He leaped off his horse, threw the reins to a man nearby, and said, "Where's Colonel Travis? Where's Jim Bowie? I saw the Mexicans!"

Someone went for the two co-commanders of the Alamo, and while everyone clustered about the scout reported that he had seen the Mexican Army and that they had crossed the Rio Grande and were heading toward San Antonio.

"It's General Santa Anna himself, coming this way," the man said. "He's leading the army—and what an army. I've never seen so many men!"

"How many?" Colonel Travis asked. "About how many men would you say?"

"Never seen so many," the scout repeated. "Thousands—"

"Thousands?" Colonel Travis asked. "You mean one thousand?"

The man took a long drink of water from a pitcher that had been handed to him. "No, sir," he said after a few thirsty gulps. "Not one thousand—looked more like six to me."

"Six thousand men!" William Barrett Travis said, laughing. "You must have been seeing things, man, or taking a long pull on some of that Mexican *tequila*."

The man shook his head and reached into the pocket of his sweat-stained jacket for a scrap of paper. On it were some pencil scratches.

"See this here," he said, translating the pencil scratches for those who crowded around. "Each long line is a division, and each short line means a brigade. Ten divisions, six brigades in each division, that's how I counted them. All right," he said stubbornly. "Let's say I counted wrong. Nine divisions, maybe, but still—"

"Still," Jim Bowie said quietly. "Between five and six thousand men headed this way."

Colonel Travis swung into action. "All right," he said. "Now that we know what to expect, we also know what to do. We divide into squads, move the ammunition, get plenty of water into the mission building. Thank goodness we've got water! We can hold out forever as long as we've got water."

"Estrella," William Bonner said, turning to his wife. "I really think—"

Estrella Bonner began to weep. "No. I won't go. I won't leave you, William."

William Bonner looked at his daughter. "Lucy," he said. "Help me."

"Ma," Lucy said. "It'll only be for a little while. Just a few days. We'll only be in the way here."

"Maybe you and Ma'd be in the way," Carlos said stubbornly, "but I'm staying here with Pa."

"No, Carlos!" Estrella Bonner shouted, her tears flowing freely now. "I will never leave without Carlos."

William Bonner looked to Lucy again.

"Carlos," Lucy said softly. "Ma and I can't manage without you. We need a man," she said to her fourteen-year-old brother. "We need you."

"I'm depending on you, Carlos," William Bonner said, but his eyes were on his daughter even as he said the words.

Lucy gave a small, hardly perceptible nod. "It's up to you to take care of us now, Carlos."

Carlos sighed. "Women," he said to his father.

William Bonner couldn't help smiling. "You're right, son. Women! What would they do without us?"

Lucy and her mother went into the mission to pack a few things. Almost everything they owned was back at the ranch, but the conversation Lucy had heard earlier was repeated once again.

"I'm leaving all the blankets for you, William."

"It'll only be a few days, Estrella."

Lucy was carrying a straw basket filled with clothes to the wagon when she saw Jesse Lee Powell.

"Lucy," he began as she brushed by him.

Lucy looked straight ahead, ignoring the tall sharp-shooter who shortened his steps to match hers.

"You've got to listen to me," he said. "There isn't much time."

Lucy turned and looked at him with contempt. "I heard all that last night."

"That idiot Harper," Jesse Lee said with some fury. "You think he could judge when a man is funning and when he means what he says?"

"Maybe he can't judge," Lucy lashed out, "but I can. 'Love me tonight for tomorrow we die.' I guess you must have taken me for pretty dumb, Mister Jesse Lee Powell, but I'm not as dumb as all that!"

"I meant every word I said," Jesse Lee said, his blue eyes beginning to sparkle with anger. "Every last dad-blamed word!"

But Lucy was unforgiving. "And if I had believed you, just how much further would you have tried to lead me on?"

"A kiss," Jesse Lee said. "That's all it would have been, I swear. One kiss to seal our love. Just one kiss, because I know we may never have a chance for another."

Lucy wanted so much to believe him that her heart begged her to give in. Still, she remained hard toward him. "Oh, you make me so mad!" she said, stamping her foot and dumping the straw basket into the Bonner wagon. "That same old story. Just one kiss, for tomorrow we die."

"And we may," Jesse Lee said soberly. "That's what may happen here at the Alamo."

Lucy pushed her heavy dark hair behind her ears. "Colonel Travis didn't sound worried, and neither did Jim Bowie, and I guess they know more about what's going on than you do, Jesse Lee Powell." Lucy surprised herself, letting the tall stranger feel the lash of her anger. "Besides," she added, "if you're so all-fired scared about what's going to happen to you here in Texas, maybe it's time you went back to Tennessee!"

"Scared? Me?" Jesse Lee was furious. "I've never been scared of anything my whole life—unless it's a pretty girl's mean talk. I won't bother you anymore, Lucy. You wouldn't believe me if'n I swore on a batch of Good Books."

"No, I wouldn't," Lucy said. "I just feel sorry for all those girls who did."

Jesse Lee's face reddened. "I do, too," he said softly, ". . . now."

Lucy was startled at Jesse Lee's admission about his past shenanigans. But what did it all mean? It was just another trick to get her to act all loving with him.

Well, fool me once, shame on you, she decided, *but fool me twice, shame on me*. And she turned back to the wagon, pretending to fuss with the straw basket. When Lucy turned around, she saw that Jesse Lee was gone and Dirk had sidled up. He leaned against the wagon, grinning at Lucy.

"What do you want?" she asked sharply.

"Your pa told my pa that you and your ma and Carlos are leaving the Alamo like us. He asked particular if me and my pa would kinda look after the three of you while he's at the Alamo. 'Course my pa said yes. Looks like we'll be seeing some of each other, Lucy."

"You won't be seeing anything of me, Dirk Shumann," Lucy said. "Besides, after last night I thought you weren't interested in marrying me."

Dirk lounged back against the wagon, and his smile was a sneer. "There are other things beside marriage," he said, "as I guess you found out from that Tennessee man."

"Dirk Shumann! Wait till I tell my pa—"

"Tell your pa what?" William Bonner asked. He had come out to the wagon with his wife holding on desperately to his arm.

Lucy looked at her father. She had never seen him look so worried. She longed to run to him and tell him how Dirk had insulted her and how Jesse Lee had lied to her, but how could she burden him now when he had so much else on his mind?

"Nothing, Pa," she said.

William Bonner nodded, too preoccupied with his wife to notice Lucy's agitation. He handed Estrella into the wagon and then turned to Dirk. "You'll look in on my family from time to time, won't you, Dirk? Give 'em a hand if they need it. I'd sure appreciate it."

"Happy to do it, Mr. Bonner," Dirk said, acting the part of the polite good neighbor. "No problem at all to ride over from our place to yours. I'll make sure to do it real often."

"Thanks, Dirk."

Lucy groaned inside, but she hugged her father and only said, "Take care of yourself, Pa. Please."

"You take care, Lucy," he said, and his eyes went to his wife, seated on the front seat of the wagon, "of everything."

"I will, Pa," Lucy said softly. "Don't you worry."

The men of the Alamo lined up beside the large wooden doors of the fort. They waved and smiled as the wagons carrying their loved ones wheeled by. There were last-minute endearments and instructions from more than a hundred men bidding goodbye to their families.

"See you in a day or two!"

"Be good, you kids. Listen to your ma."

"Don't forget to move them cows up to the north pasture, Billy. But don't start work on the new barn till I get back."

The women and children in the wagons smiled and waved back, and Estrella Bonner managed a last loving smile at her husband. It was only when they were on the dirt road that led out of San Antonio to their ranch that she began to cry softly. "I don't know why we couldn't have stayed with your father," she said. "Some of the women stayed."

"Very few of them, Ma," Lucy reminded her. "And Colonel Travis said it would be easier if the men could concentrate on the Mexicans without having to worry about their families."

"I wouldn't have been any trouble," Estrella said. Lucy didn't say anything.

They were quiet as they rode out. Then, after a few moments, Estrella looked at her daughter and admitted, "I probably would have been the most trouble of all. Your father was right to make us go, Lucy."

Lucy put her arm around her mother's shoulder. She loved her mother; she especially loved how her mother was able to face the truth about herself. And Lucy had faith, too—faith that told her that in a real emergency her mother would be able to cope.

Lucy knew that she was a lot like her mother. She was quiet and shy, but she had the strength not to let anyone push her around, especially men like Dirk Shumann and that Jesse Lee Powell!

The wagons moved in a slow line away from San Antonio and away from the Alamo. Carlos stirred restlessly in the back of the wagon.

"It'll be good to get back to the ranch and our horses," he said. "I hate this slow old wagon."

Lucy agreed. She'd been riding since she was five. She loved packing a lunch and riding out to a far corner of the Bonner ranch by herself. She always had a good excuse for these solitary rides—a missing heifer that had wandered off, a message that had to be carried to a neighbor—any excuse that gave her the chance for a day's ride in open country would do.

Lucy clicked to the horses that were pulling the wagon, wishing with Carlos that they could move a little faster. She thought about her white mare, Blanca, and that tomorrow she would be riding her. She closed her eyes for a second, and she could almost hear the sound of rocks and clods of dirt flying out from beneath Blanca's hooves.

She actually thought she heard the sound—imagination was remarkable—but then Lucy shook her head. It wasn't her imagination; there was a rider coming from behind, passing the row of slowly moving wagons.

"Carlos," Lucy called to her brother. "Can you see anything?"

Carlos tried to see past the wagons behind them. "One rider, and he's moving fast."

"Something's happened," Estrella said fearfully. "Something's happened back at the Alamo."

"Couldn't be, Ma," Lucy said. "We just left there an hour or so ago. Nothing could have happened. Carlos, can you make him out? Who is it?"

"I can't tell," Carlos answered. "Whoever it is, he's moving so fast he's throwing up a cloud of dust. He'll pass us in minutes, Lucy. We'll see who it is then."

The horses pulling the Bonner wagon became slightly agitated as the sound of the lone horseman came steadily nearer, and Lucy had to pull back on the reins to control them.

"That rider has lost his senses," Lucy said to her mother and brother. "He's frightening the horses." She pulled back hard on the reins and wished she were wearing gloves as she felt the leather bite into her fingers. "Whoa! Hold on there."

The rider pulled up beside the wagon and slowed his horse to a dancing canter, then to a nervous walk. "Lucy," Jesse Lee Powell said. "I couldn't let you go like that. I—" He stopped and tipped his wide-brimmed hat to a startled Estrella Bonner. "How do, ma'am," he said. Then he turned back to Lucy. "I couldn't let you go thinking that I didn't mean what I said. I—"

"Lucy," her mother asked. "Who is this young man?"

"Ma, it's no one important."

"My name's Jesse Lee Powell, ma'am, and I'm really pleased to make your acquaintance."

"Hi, Jesse Lee," Carlos said, bouncing up from the back of the wagon.

Jesse Lee grinned. "How're you doing, Charlie?"

"Charlie?" Estrella Bonner asked. "Charlie?"

"Jesse Lee never met anyone called Carlos, Ma, so I told him to call me Charlie."

"Lucy," Jesse Lee began again. "You've got to listen to me, Lucy."

"Not now," Lucy said, aware of her mother's shocked curiosity and the fact that Carlos was listening to every word that was being said. "Not here."

"It better be here and now, Lucy. I may not have another chance."

"Not that again," Lucy said angrily. "Not that same old story."

"It's a story that may not have a happy ending," Jesse Lee persisted. "And if it doesn't, I wanted you to have something to remember me by."

"Oh, I'll remember you all right."

"Take this, Lucy," Jesse Lee said, holding something shiny and golden out to her. "It belonged to another woman I loved."

The nerve of the man! Why, he was nothing but a *blamed* backwoodsman. "I don't want anything from you," she said.

Lucy's deep, dark eyes revealed her anger, but with one sweet smile Jesse Lee was able to push it aside. "My mother, Lucy. It belonged to my ma. Now take it and find a way to trust in me. There's not much time."

Estrella Bonner had watched the two young people long enough. It was time she intervened. "When did you meet my daughter, Mr. Powell?" she asked, aware of the unconventional nature of the situation.

"Call me Jesse Lee, ma'am, please. Lucy—"

Lucy was a bit calmer but still felt the need to harden herself against the handsome sharpshooter. After all, she had determined just last night that all she wanted was to be an old maid. "I told you—"

"I know what you told me. Whoa!" Jesse Lee

pulled his horse up. "But you got to stop being such a mule, Lucy. Now here. It was my ma's, and I want you to have it." He took her left hand, opened her tightly clenched fingers, and placed the shiny gold object in the palm of her hand.

"Got to get back to the fort," he said, turning his horse around. "Davy'll skin me alive if he finds out I rode off like this. Real nice meeting you, ma'am," he said to Estrella Bonner. "Be seein' you, Charlie. Lucy, I meant every word—*every* word." And with that Jesse Lee Powell wheeled, heading back to the Alamo, leaving a wake of dust behind him.

Lucy half turned in her seat, but she couldn't see him. She was shaking as she turned back. She gripped the reins with her right hand, opening her left. It was a half-moon locket. His mother's. He had called her a mule and given her a delicate gold locket in the shape of a half-moon. The locket was etched with silver and suspended from a thin gold chain.

"Lucy," Estrella Bonner said. "When we get back home, we'll have a little talk."

"Yes, Ma," Lucy said, groaning inwardly. She knew her mother's little talks—they resembled the questioning of the Spanish Inquisition.

"I like Jesse Lee," Carlos said cheerfully. "He promised to take me squirrel hunting after he takes care of Santa Anna."

"We don't have many squirrels in Texas," Estrella Bonner said. "And I'll have a little talk with you, too, Carlos. *Charlie!* What an idea!"

Chapter 4

LUCY WAS SORRY HER FATHER HAD EVER ASKED DIRK Shumann to give the Bonners a hand with their ranch. It's true that they were short-handed—most of the hands had stayed on at the Alamo—but Lucy would rather have worked around the clock than have Dirk Shumann constantly about.

"My ma told me to ride over," Dirk would say, all mealy-mouthed, to Estrella Bonner. "She said you people might need a little help."

"That's good of you, Dirk," Lucy's mother said the first two or three times he had come to their ranch. But Estrella Bonner was no fool—she saw the way her daughter slipped from the room whenever Dirk Shumann stopped by.

It was just as well that her mother hadn't been in the barn when Lucy was giving Blanca a rubdown and

Dirk came looking for her. "Need any help, Lucy?" he said, edging around the stall. "Want me to do that for you?"

"No thanks, Dirk. Blanca doesn't like strangers touching her."

Dirk grinned a mean, evil grin. "Doesn't take after you, does she, Lucy?"

Lucy reached for the riding crop that was hanging from a nail outside the stall. "Don't you dare talk to me that way, Dirk Shumann."

Dirk caught her hand before she was able to reach the riding crop. "Quiet, little Lucy," he said. "I never knew you had such a temper. But then I didn't know a lot of things about you."

Lucy was getting ready to scream when Blanca lashed out with a rear hoof and caught Dirk squarely on the left shin. Dirk yelped in pain and moved back away from Blanca.

"Get out of here," Lucy said, the crop now in her hand. "And stay away from me and from Blanca."

Dirk hobbled to the barn door. "That's the thanks a fella gets for trying to help out a helpless woman."

Lucy laughed and took a few steps toward him, her riding crop raised. "Not all that helpless, best you remember that."

When she got back to the house, her mother questioned her. "Was that Dirk Shumann, Lucy? Again?"

Lucy nodded. "He wanted to know if he could do something to help, Ma. I told him we didn't need any help."

Estrella Bonner nodded. "I'm glad you said that, Lucy. If Mr. Shumann and Dirk had wanted to do something to help, they should have stayed at the Alamo with the other men. That's where their help was needed."

Carlos, who had been sitting quietly at the bleached white pine table, said, "I don't like Dirk. There's something about him, I don't know what exactly."

Estrella and Lucy looked at each other over Carlos's head, and Lucy said, "I don't think we'll be seeing quite so much of him anymore."

Later that night, when she was in bed but still wide awake, Lucy heard the sound of a horse's hooves coming down the dirt road from the direction of the Shumann ranch. Lucy threw open the window and looked out. There wasn't much of a moon, but she could make out the figure of one rider barreling down the road toward the Bonner ranch.

"Lucy," Estrella said, coming into her daughter's room. "Who could that be?"

"I don't know, Ma."

Carlos appeared in his night clothes. "Probably Dirk," he said. "Come to court Lucy by moonlight."

"It had better not be Dirk Shumann," Estrella said angrily. "He'll be greeted with my father's pistol if he's come in the middle of the night with any such ideas. Just because William isn't at home doesn't mean he can try and take advantage of our circumstances."

"Oh, Ma," Lucy said. "He's probably bringing

news. Maybe the Shumanns heard something from the Alamo. Their ranch is close to the crossroads."

"Put a robe on, Lucy," Estrella ordered. "We'll just see what this midnight visit is about."

The three Bonners were standing on their wide colonnade porch when the rider pulled up. There was hardly any moon at all this night, but something in the way the rider carried himself on his horse made Lucy's head whirl.

"Whoa there, old son," they heard a voice say. "Easy now."

"It's Jesse Lee!" Carlos let out a shout as he took the porch steps two at a time. But Lucy didn't need Carlos to tell her what her heart had already seen.

"Hey, Charlie! How're you doing, boy?"

"Jesse Lee," Lucy called out, following her brother. Estrella Bonner was behind them, saying, "Charlie . . . why must it be Charlie?"

The three crowded around Jesse Lee. He stretched out, nearly lying down on his horse's neck, and Lucy could see that both he and his mount were plainly exhausted.

Jesse Lee raised his well-worn, wide-brimmed hat to Estrella. "Evening, ma'am. Sorry to come by so late in the night. Is it all right if I step down from my horse, ma'am? He's one tired animal."

"Mr. Powell," Estrella said. "Please dismount and come into the house. Lucy, some coffee. Carlos, take care of Mr. Powell's horse."

Her mother had remembered Jesse Lee's name, Lucy thought, smiling to herself as she hurried back into the house. Maybe no one else noticed it, but Lucy was aware of her mother's convenient memory. Estrella Bonner never remembered the names of people she didn't like.

Jesse Lee followed the Bonner women into the house. He sat down in a kitchen chair, his long booted legs stretched out before him.

"Been riding close to twenty-four hours," he said, rubbing his eyes. "Maybe some of that coffee'll help me go on."

"Twenty-four hours!" Estrella Bonner exclaimed. "What's happened?"

Lucy turned from the kitchen range, watching Jesse Lee as he talked. He was so exhausted that his words were slurred. She wanted to reach out and push his thick honey-colored hair away from his forehead. She longed to bring a footstool to prop up those dusty booted feet, but she forced herself to remain a few feet away from him and to do nothing more than listen.

"They've come," Jesse Lee was saying, all the while keeping his eyes on Lucy. "Santy Anny and what looks like the whole Mexican Army. Colonel Travis sent me out last night—it was pretty dark—sent me to Fort Goliad."

"Where is Santa Anna?" Lucy asked, her back still against the kitchen range. "Has he attacked the Alamo?"

Jesse Lee shook his head. "No, not yet, but they're

camped a mile or so down the road. That's why Colonel Travis sent me to Fort Goliad."

"Why did he send you to Fort Goliad?" Lucy asked. "I don't understand."

"Sent me to see General Fannin," Jesse Lee mumbled. "Sent me for help." Jesse Lee's eyes closed, and his chin rested on his chest.

Lucy moved forward, and she shook him gently. "Jesse Lee, please tell us. Is the general going to send help?"

Jesse Lee's eyes opened, and he tried to sit up. "Can't," he said. "General Fannin said he had to wait on word from Sam Houston. Said he had to wait." Jesse Lee took Lucy's hand, which had been resting on his shoulder. Her hand in his felt natural and just right. "The general wanted me to catch a couple of hours of sleep in Goliad, but I told him I couldn't. Told him I had to see my girl—one last time."

"Oh Jesse." Lucy's eyes filled with tears. "Don't— don't say such things."

Jesse Lee smiled a sweet crooked grin. "Know you don't like me saying such things, Lucy. Know you don't believe it."

Lucy was crying openly. "But that's not true anymore. I'm beginning to believe it . . . now."

"Lucy," Estrella Bonner said gently. "Take Mr. Powell to the front room. "He'll be more comfortable there. I'll bring the coffee."

"Come on, Jesse Lee." Lucy held her hand out to him. "I'll help you."

Jesse Lee put his arm around Lucy's shoulders and pretended to lean on her. There was a shadow of the charming and wicked Jesse Lee in his smile when he said, "Can't refuse an offer like that, Miss Lucy."

Lucy led Jesse Lee into the parlor, and he groaned as he sat down on the soft cushion of the front room's best settee. "Feels good after being in that saddle for so long," he said as he leaned back, his eyes closing. "If I could just get me twenty winks."

Lucy sat quietly beside him until her mother came in with a tray on which she had placed the coffee pot and coffee cups—their silver coffee pot, Lucy noticed, and their best cups.

"I don't think we should wake him," Lucy whispered.

"I'm awake," Jesse Lee said, sitting up. "That coffee smells mighty good. A pot of that and I'll be ready to ride again."

"Do you have to leave so quickly?" Estrella said. "Perhaps a few hours sleep—"

"Can't do that, ma'am. They're waiting for me back at the Alamo. Got to let them know they can't expect help from General Fannin, leastways not yet."

"Do you think they'll attack?" Estrella asked fearfully. "Do you think General Santa Anna will attack the Alamo?"

Jesse Lee looked at her, and as tired as he was he realized how worried she was about her husband. "I don't think so, ma'am," he told her. "I don't think they have to. I figure old Santy Anny will just sit there and try and starve us out, and before he can do that we're bound to get some help from Sam Houston."

"I'm going back with you," Carlos said, walking into the room. "When you ride back to the Alamo, Jesse Lee, I'm going with you."

"Carlos," his mother said sharply. "I don't want to hear such nonsense. Go to bed." Estrella looked at her daughter and Jesse Lee. "And I will go upstairs, too. Lucy, pour some more coffee, and call me, please, before Mr. Powell leaves."

"Please, ma'am—Jesse Lee."

Estrella smiled. "Jesse Lee, of course. Call me before Jesse Lee leaves, Lucy. I'm going to make a small package of a few things to send to your father." Estrella looked worriedly at Jesse Lee. "It wouldn't be too much for you to carry back just a small package, would it, Jesse Lee?"

The slow, sweet smile that Lucy had seen every night in her dreams adorned his face. "Now, I'd carry back the moon for you, Mrs. Bonner, if I could."

Estrella was charmed by the young man's words. "Thank you, Jesse Lee. It would mean so much. Come, Carlos," she said as she shepherded her son before her and closed the door to the front room behind them.

"Your ma's nice," Jesse Lee said sleepily.

Lucy smiled. "She'd charmed by you. We all are."

Jesse Lee grinned. "Or maybe she knows I'm too

tired to try for a kiss. 'Course, if you'd just lean forward a touch, Lucy, I think I could be able to manage—"

But then he was instantly serious and there was no resisting him. Dark circles gave his blue eyes the depth of black sapphires. "Lucy, this battle is making things happen so quick. I know you're brave enough for me to tell you that no matter what I told your ma, I don't know if we're going to make it out there. If anything happens to me, I want it to be with the memory of your sweet kiss on my lips."

Lucy didn't allow herself time to think about what he was saying. Instead she leaned forward. She wanted to kiss Jesse Lee, wanted to have the memory of that kiss as much as he did. She bent toward him, since he was too weary to hold her in his arms. Their lips touched, as light as feathers, as soft as flowers. That's all there was, and afterward Lucy took a deep breath. She was trembling.

"I know," Jesse Lee said, taking her hand and bringing it to his lips. "I know. I love you, Lucy."

He was still holding her hand when his eyes shut, and his head dropped to one side and rested against her shoulder. Lucy sat there with him, not moving, never wanting these stolen, precious moments to end. Jesse Lee slept, Lucy wasn't sure for how long. She didn't dare move for fear of disturbing him.

Jesse Lee woke with a start. He sat up, but he still didn't release Lucy's hand. "Have I been asleep for long?" he asked.

"I don't think so," she said gently. "Besides, you needed the sleep."

Jesse Lee smiled. "It was a sweet sleep because I had a sweet dream. Was it a dream, Lucy, that kiss?"

Lucy blushed and shook her head. "No dream, Jesse Lee."

He kissed her fingertips and let go of her hand. "Didn't think so," he said. "Never had a dream that good." He sat up and took a big watch out of his waistcoat pocket. He flipped open the lid and whistled when he saw that he had slept for a whole hour.

He had rumpled his hair in his sleep, and the thoughts she was having made Lucy look down to her hands, clasped tightly in her lap—hands that yearned to touch his hair, his cheek. Lucy's own bold thoughts embarrassed her. She could feel her blush starting, ready to give her away, and she kept her head down.

"I better be starting," he said. Then Jesse Lee placed one gentle finger under her chin, ordering her dark eyes to meet his. "My sweet, shy Lucy. How I wish we had more time."

"You'll come back, won't you?" Lucy asked, suddenly frightened, remembering what he had said to her last night. "You'll be all right?"

"Why, sure. Come on now, aren't you the girl who doesn't believe the line about 'Give me a kiss tonight, for tomorrow I die'?"

"That was before," Lucy said sadly. "Now I do believe it."

"Nothing's going to happen to me—I promise you. I'm planning to come back here and marry the rancher's daughter. A girl as pretty as you—you don't think I'd be fool enough to let old Santy Anny hurt me when I got you to come back to, do you, Lucy?"

"*Santa Anna*," Lucy said, somewhere between laughter and tears. "It's *Santa Anna*."

"Who cares? Only one name you got to worry about remembering, Lucy, and that's Mrs. Jesse Lee Powell. I hope you like the sound of it."

"I love it," Lucy said, and the next thing she knew she was in Jesse Lee's arms and he was holding her close.

"I do believe I'm feeling better," he said, kissing the tip of her nose. "I think I've gotten my strength back. Maybe even enough strength to give you a proper kiss—"

The door to the front room opened, and Estrella Bonner stood there. "Lucy—"

"I'm sorry, Ma, but—"

"I'm the one who's sorry, ma'am," Jesse Lee interrupted. "But that old Santy Anny just doesn't give a man the time to do things right. I know I should've spoken to you first, but I've asked Miss Lucy to marry me."

To Lucy's surprise, Estrella Bonner smiled, but her eyes showed a mother's concern. "The two of you are moving too quickly," she said.

Jesse Lee nodded. It was amazing to Lucy how well this easy-going backwoodsman got along with her formal mother. "Well, ma'am, after we get rid of Santy Anny, I want to come back and court Lucy all proper-like."

"Come back soon, Jesse Lee," Estrella Bonner said.

"I'll do that, ma'am," Jesse Lee said.

Lucy and Jesse Lee walked out of the house slowly, their arms around each other. Carlos had saddled Jesse Lee's horse, and he said once again, "I wish I was going with you, Jesse Lee."

"You got to take care of the women, Charlie," Jesse Lee said. "I'm depending on you."

Estrella Bonner put her arm about her son. "Come on, Carlos," she said. "Let's go inside."

Jesse Lee and Lucy stood in the front yard and watched the sky streak with red and then orange as the sun came up.

"You sure got beautiful skies in Texas," Jesse Lee said. "A man can see almost to tomorrow."

"Tomorrow," Lucy whispered. "What do you think'll happen tomorrow?"

"I think Santy Anny is going to realize that he's better off turning tail and going home. He's bound to do that when Sam Houston sends a passel of men. And then I'm going to ride like lightning and come back here to my Lucy girl."

"Oh, Jesse Lee." Lucy couldn't help the sob that welled up in her throat. "Jesse Lee—"

He took her in his arms and they clung to each other. Finally, Jesse Lee pushed Lucy almost roughly from him. He mounted his horse and leaned down from the saddle.

"I'll be back, Lucy," he told her, and then his mouth burned a kiss upon her lips.

"*Dios quiere,*" Lucy whispered as she watched him ride off. "God willing. Oh yes, please, *Dios quiere.*"

Chapter 5

LUCY STAYED OUTSIDE UNTIL SHE COULD NO LONGER see Jesse Lee. *Keep him safe*, she prayed. *Dear Lord, I love him so. Keep him safe.*

She went back to the house, and, moving quietly so as not to disturb her mother, she went into her room and threw herself on top of her bed. She hadn't realized how exhausted she was, and she fell asleep almost immediately. When she woke more than a hour later it was with a start. What was she doing lying on top of the bed covers? And then she remembered, and the prayer came to her mind once again. *Keep Jesse Lee safe. Dear Lord, keep him safe.*

Lucy washed, changed into a fresh dress, and went downstairs. Her mother had the coffee pot perking on the large iron range, and she gave Lucy a warm hug.

"I like your young man," Estrella said. "He reminds me of your father."

"Pa?" Lucy was surprised.

"Pa?" Estrella mimicked her. "He wasn't always your pa. When he courted me he was very much like Jesse Lee—bold, daring . . ." Now Estrella peered knowingly at her daughter. "And handsome."

Lucy blushed. "That sounds like Jesse Lee, all right."

Estrella placed cups on the large table. "It's time Carlos was up. Get him, please, Lucy."

Lucy went out to the center hall and called to her brother. When he didn't answer, she ran up the stairs and tapped on his door.

"Oh bother," she said when he still didn't answer, and she opened the door to his room impatiently. "Carlos—"

But Carlos wasn't there. Lucy looked around and saw a scrawled note on a piece of paper on Carlos's pillow.

I am following Jesse Lee to the Alamo, the note read. *I want to be with Pa. Don't worry, Ma, I'll be all right*. The note was signed *Charlie*.

Lucy ran down the stairs and into the kitchen. "Ma," she said. "Ma—"

Lucy hadn't realized that her mother had been forcing herself to stay calm for her children's sake, but the news that Carlos had left for the fort was too much for her. She started to cry—the sobs seemed to come from so deep within her that Lucy trembled to hear them.

"Ma, please," Lucy said, leading her mother to a chair. She grasped her mother's hands between her own. "I'll go after Carlos. I'll bring him back and—"

"No!" Estrella Bonner said quickly. "Don't leave me, Lucy. I'm afraid for you."

"I'll be all right, Ma."

"You can't go to the Alamo. There's fighting—"

"Not yet there isn't," Lucy said. "You heard Jesse Lee. Right now Santa Anna is trying to starve them out. I'll go and get Carlos, Ma, that's all. I'll be all right."

"I don't know." Estrella buried her head in her hands. "I don't know what to do anymore. First your father, now Carlos, and you."

"I'll bring Carlos back," Lucy repeated. "And we'll be together when Pa comes back."

"If he comes back," Estrella said, unable to control her weeping. "I don't know how much more I can stand, Lucy."

Lucy kneeled beside her mother's chair. "You'll feel better when Carlos is home."

Estrella sat up and made an effort to control herself. "Yes," she whispered, her dark eyes wide with fear. "At least—at least bring Carlos back."

"Ma," Lucy said. "Maybe you should stay with the Shumanns until I get back."

"No!" Estrella gripped the edge of the table as

though she was afraid that Lucy was going to try and drag her forcibly out of the house. "No. I'll wait for you here. For you and for Carlos. I want to wait here—at home."

"All right, Ma, all right," Lucy said, and she stroked her mother's hair. Estrella was so agitated that Lucy hated to leave her alone. She would ask Ramiro's wife to stay in the house until she returned, and she would also stop at the Shumann ranch and ask Greta Shumann to look in on her mother.

It took Lucy only minutes to get ready. She donned the wide-legged divided skirt, the shirt, and the short jacket she wore when she rode around the ranch, and she knotted a large white square about her throat. She pulled her shining dark hair back into a bun and took a flat-crowned, narrow-brimmed black hat from the wardrobe shelf.

Lucy left the house dressed in an outfit similiar to what a Mexican *vaquero* wore when he rode at special rodeos, and after asking Paco, Ramiro's son, to saddle Blanca, she arranged for María Ramiro to stay with her mother.

Lucy went into the house to say goodbye to her mother. Estrella had left the kitchen and was staring out the window of the front room—the window that looked out on the straight road that led away from the ranch house.

"Ma," Lucy said softly.

Estrella did her best to smile. "I'll be all right, Lucy. Come back as soon as you can—you and Carlos."

Lucy mounted Blanca and rode away from the ranch. When she reached the main road she turned in her saddle and waved toward the house. She couldn't see if her mother was sitting by the window, but she was sure that she was, so Lucy took her hat off and waved that too.

Lucy turned down the main road, and she didn't stop until she came to the Shumann ranch. All three Shumanns came out of the house, but Lucy refused their invitation to come inside. "No time," she said. She explained her mission, asking Mrs. Shumann to look in on her mother.

"Of course," Greta Shumann said. "I'll ride over right now. But Lucy, will you be safe? You just said that Santa Anna and his army are camped right outside San Antonio."

"I'll be fine," Lucy said. "Not everybody's left San Antonio. Things can't be that bad."

"That's crazy," Dirk said, and for a minute Lucy thought he was going to offer to escort her to the fort. But he said, "You're a fool to go, Lucy, and so was Carlos."

"Dirk!" Greta Shumann's voice was sharp. "Lucy knows what she's doing. It's bad enough for Estrella that Will's at the Alamo. She doesn't need the extra worry about Carlos. Go ahead, Lucy, but take care. I'll go see your ma right away."

Lucy rode away from the Shumann ranch, and this time she didn't turn back to wave. She kept Blanca at an even trot, and as she rode she tried to plan on what she would do *if.*

Ever since she was a little girl, Lucy had tried to plan out her ifs. *If* this happens, I'll do this. *If* that happens, I'll do the other. *If* Dirk asks me to dance, I'll say I sprained my ankle. *If* Ma says it's too hot to go riding, I'll try not to answer sassy, but maybe she'll let me go *if* I say I want to take Pa his lunch.

But now the ifs that faced her were more complicated! *If* I run into the Mexican Army, *if* I see Jesse Lee at the fort—but no, that wasn't an *if*, that was a *when*. There was no question she would see Jesse Lee, and her heart began to beat faster at the thought of it.

Was she riding to the Alamo to bring back Carlos, or was she making this dangerous journey to see Jesse Lee? Lucy smiled and moved Blanca into a canter. She had to admit the truth: it was a little of both.

Lucy slowed Blanca down to a walk when she came close to San Antonio. If she did run into anyone from the Mexican Army, she didn't want them to know that she was riding to the Alamo. She was just another San Antonian out for a ride to exercise her horse.

Lucy adjusted her hat, pulled her jacket straight, and hoped that neither she nor Blanca showed the effects of their long, dusty ride. It was silly to worry or feel afraid, she decided. After all, Jesse Lee had ridden out of the Alamo, and he wasn't worried about getting back to the fort.

It was only after a Mexican lieutenant and four of his men rode up and surrounded her that she remembered that Jesse Lee was a frontier scout. He had traveled through Indian territory with safety, while she hadn't even been able to sneak into San Antonio without being stopped by the enemy.

Lucy tried to bluff her way past the men of the Mexican Army. She spoke to them in Spanish and told them that she had just gone out for a short ride—her horse needed the exercise—and now she was riding to her home in the city of San Antonio.

The lieutenant ordered his men to stay close to Lucy. Then he turned his full attention on her, looking like a cat playing with a helpless little mouse. Even in the midst of her fear, Lucy noticed that when he spoke to her he addressed her in English.

"Your horse is lathered, and your clothes show the dust of many miles, *señorita*. It's clear that you're not from San Antonio. You've ridden far—from the fort at Goliad, perhaps? Carrying a message for the commanders of the Alamo?"

Lucy sat up a little straighter and put a calming hand on Blanca, who was made nervous by the soldiers and horses crowding about her.

"That's a foolish idea," she said, forcing herself to speak slowly, her voice casual. "I don't know about any message. Besides, General Fannin would hardly send a girl—" Lucy bit her lips. The moment she said it, she realized it had been a mistake to mention the general.

"You know his name," the lieutenant said. "The general's name. A girl, yes, and perhaps a spy."

59

"I'm no spy," Lucy said, and her voice rose.

"Maybe not," the lieutenant said as he spurred his horse closer to her. "But I'll just see for myself if you're carrying a message." He reached out to pull the jacket from Lucy's shoulders.

"No!" Lucy shouted, and at the sound of her voice Blanca reared straight up, her front hooves pawing the air.

Lucy leaned forward quickly, gripped Blanca's flanks with her knees, and managed to stay in the saddle.

"Blanca, it's all right," she said, calming the frightened animal. "Nothing to be afraid of."

The lieutenant looked with admiration at the slim girl. She could ride, she could speak Spanish, and she was brave—too bad she wasn't on the Mexican side.

"It's not the horse that has to be afraid, *señorita.* Mexicans are kind to animals."

"And not to women?" Lucy stared him directly in the face, nearly challenging him. She was surprised by her own boldness and the ease with which she was able to snap back an answer at the lieutenant. She had always heard that people find courage in moments of danger, and it was true. Now she even found the strength to tease him. "I'm disappointed," she said. "My mother's family comes from Mexico, and I was always told that Mexican gentlemen are gallant to women."

"Your family is Mexican—of course," the lieutenant smiled at last. "That explains it."

"Explains what?"

The lieutenant took off his hat and bowed slightly to Lucy. "Your charm, your bravery, and your beauty."

I've won, Lucy thought exultantly. *I've won. He won't stop me now from reaching the Alamo.* But she had misread the lieutenant, because when she smiled and tried to ride past him, he moved forward, forcing her to rein Blanca to a halt.

"Not so quickly, *señorita,* not so quickly. General Santa Anna would be happy to meet such a lovely Anglo-Mexican."

"I'm a Texan," Lucy said.

"A Texan?" The lieutenant's eyebrows went up. "And just what is that, *señorita?* This Texas territory belongs to Mexico."

It does now, Lucy longed to say, *but maybe not for always. Soon we will be the Republic of Texas.* Instead, she smiled and answered, "Let's just say I'm a San Antonian. A San Antonian who would like to get home."

The lieutenant was polite but immovable. "I'm sure the general will be happy to give you an escort so that you can get home safely—after you meet him."

There was nothing Lucy could do. The lieutenant rode beside her, and two of his men rode in front while two rode behind them.

Lucy did her best to remain calm. She wasn't a spy, after all, and she was breaking no laws, not even any laws that General Santa Anna might have devised. As far as she knew, he hadn't issued any orders demanding that all San Antonians stay in their homes. She was just out for a ride. Of course, she knew it was a ride to the Alamo—the fort that the general and his army had under siege.

She was afraid. She just hoped that her fear didn't show. She sat up a little straighter in her saddle.

Let me do this right, she prayed. *Let me do nothing that would make Pa or Jesse Lee ashamed of me. I'm a Texan,* she kept saying over and over to herself. *And Texans aren't afraid—not of anything.*

Chapter 6

LUCY DID HER BEST TO MAINTAIN HER ERECT POS-
ture as the lieutenant escorted her through the lines of
the Mexican Army to General Santa Anna's command
tent, but she couldn't help stealing a look around her
as she rode.

She had never seen so many men gathered in one
place. Santa Anna's army was huge. There were rows
of tents, corrals filled with horses, more cannons than
she knew existed. Lucy thought of the small group of
men at the Alamo, and her heart hammered with
fear—and this time the fear was stronger because it
wasn't for herself. Pa, Jesse Lee, Carlos—what was
going to happen to them? Did they know how large an
army faced them? If she could only get to the Alamo to
warn them!

The lieutenant and his men halted in front of a large

tent, and Lucy saw that two flags were flying above the tent pole—the red, white, and green flag of Mexico and another smaller flag that was bright red.

One of the men held Lucy's horse, and the lieutenant insisted on helping her dismount.

She waited outside the tent, surrounded by the lieutenant's soldiers, who looked at her curiously. Minutes later the lieutenant came out and escorted her into the tent.

A haughty-looking man with a small beard and shifting dark eyes sat behind a small, elaborately carved wooden desk. When he saw Lucy, he stood. Lucy noticed the gold epaulets on the shoulders of his uniform and the medals pinned to his jacket.

"General," the lieutenant said nervously. "This is—this is—*señorita,* what is your name?"

"I'm Lucy Bonner."

"Bonner," General Santa Anna repeated, looking disappointed. "I thought you said that this young lady was of our blood." He spoke in Spanish, and Lucy answered him in his own language.

"My mother's family is from Mexico," she said. "They came from Spain originally."

"Your mother?" The General brightened to hear Lucy speak in Spanish. "And what is her name?"

"Estrella Morales y Fuentes."

The general nodded appreciatively. "Then you are Señorita Bonner y Morales-Fuentes," he said, adding her mother's name to her usual surname. "This is how you would be called in Mexico. This is how you will be called here after we teach these arrogant Texans some manners."

Lucy tired to smile. "I know nothing about such things, General."

The general smiled in return, and he answered her in English. "Of course, that is clear. You know nothing of what is happening at the Alamo. You were just out for an afternoon's ride on your horse, isn't that so?"

Lucy swallowed hard. She wanted to lie—tried hard to lie—but it was obvious that the general wouldn't believe any simple-minded lie, so she decided to take a big chance and tell him the truth. "I was riding to the Alamo," she said, "but I'm no spy."

The general looked at her shrewdly. "No?" he asked. "Why would a pretty young woman go riding through a countryside filled with soldiers unless she was a spy? Do you have an answer for that, *señorita?*"

"I do," Lucy said, "and it's the truth. My father's at the Alamo, and my brother Carlos left our ranch this morning to join him. My mother is frantic. I'm going to the Alamo to bring Carlos back."

"Carlos," the general repeated softly. "And how old is this Carlos?"

"Fourteen," Lucy said. "He's only fourteen."

The general stared at her quietly for a moment. "If Carlos has your courage, Señorita Lucy Bonner y Morales-Fuentes, we would like to have him on our side."

"Carlos is too young to be on any side," Lucy began, but then she realized that those words were a betrayal of Carlos, and her father, and Jesse Lee, so once again she decided to tell the truth. "Besides, he's a Texan, and we have our own side."

The general shook his head and then led Lucy outside the tent. He pointed to the two flags that were waving gently in the mild breeze. "Does that mean anything to you, *señorita?*"

"That's the flag of Mexico," Lucy answered. "But the red flag—I don't recognize it."

The general looked at her, his face serious. "It's the flag that means *no quarter.*"

"What? I don't understand."

"No quarter. It means that there will be no prisoners taken at the Alamo. If the men at the Alamo fight, it will be to the death—their death. I will let you go to the Alamo, *señorita,* and you will bring the men there my message: Absolute surrender or death."

Lucy shivered. It wasn't a cold day, but she couldn't help herself—she was shivering beneath a warm sun.

The general had noticed, and he nodded. "You are young," he told her, "but I can see you understand. Tell the men of the Alamo that General Santa Anna flies the red flag of death, and tell them, too, what you have seen here."

Lucy knew what he meant as she looked about her. The Mexican Army was spread out over acres—men, arms, horses—as far as the eye could see.

"I'll tell them," she whispered, doing her best to keep her voice steady. "But I don't think—" and she didn't dare finish her sentence.

Santa Anna nodded. He knew what it was that Lucy yearned to tell him—that not even an army twice the size of his would make the men of the Alamo give up. "It is too bad," he said, his voice so low that only Lucy heard him. "So young and so beautiful—and about to suffer so much. Your father and your brother are both at the Alamo. Is there anyone else there whom you love, *señorita?*"

Lucy faced him. "Yes," she said. "There is someone there that I love very much."

"Then tell him," the general said. "For your own sake, tell him about the red flag." He shook his head. "You are on the wrong side, *señorita*, I am sorry for you and for your mother."

Lucy bit her lips and stopped herself from saying anything more to the general. He turned from her, spoke to the lieutenant in Spanish, ordering him to escort Lucy through the army lines.

Lucy mounted, and she and the lieutenant rode slowly past the battalions. Lucy would have preferred to ride away from the Mexican Army quickly, but the lieutenant wouldn't have it. Lucy realized that Santa Anna had told the lieutenant to make sure that she saw the might of the Mexican Army. He wanted her to tell the men at the Alamo what she had seen. Perhaps if they knew the strength of his forces, they would give up.

When they came to the last of the army lines, Lucy could see the Alamo in the distance.

"You will be safe now," the lieutenant said. "The Alamo isn't very far away."

"I'll be safe," Lucy echoed.

"For a while," the lieutenant said softly. "But don't stay at the Alamo too long, *señorita*." He saluted Lucy, wheeled his horse about, and rode away.

This time Lucy put her spurs to Blanca, and, leaning forward in her saddle, she urged her horse to a gallop.

"Rider coming, rider coming!" she heard the sentry shout from the top of the stone wall. "One rider—one rider—coming through! Open the gates!"

When Lucy and Blanca reached the wall, the wide gates swung back, and still at a gallop she rode into the courtyard of the Alamo.

"It's Lucy!" she heard a man shout. "Somebody get Will Bonner."

"Lucy!" The men of the Alamo surrounded her horse, and eager hands helped her dismount. "How did you get through the Mexican lines?"

Before Lucy could answer, her father pushed through the crowd of men. "Lucy," he said, sweeping her to him. "Are you all right?"

"Pa!" Lucy hugged her father. "Pa, I'm so glad to see you."

William Bonner held his daughter by the shoulders. "Lucy, it's your ma, isn't it?" he said. "Something's happened to your ma."

"No, no, Ma's all right. But she was worried about Carlos. I've come to get him, Pa. He's got to come home with me."

Jim Bowie had pushed through the circle of excited people. "You rode right past old Santa Anna and his Mexicans just to get your brother?" he asked. His eyes gleamed with admiration. "That's real Texas spirit for you!"

"I didn't exactly ride *past* General Santa Anna," Lucy said. "I saw him. He gave me a message."

"A message from old Santa Anna," Jim Bowie's voice boomed over the courtyard. "Says he's ready to give up, does he?"

Lucy looked searchingly at all the smiling, eager faces around her. Where was Jesse Lee? And how could she tell these people about Santa Anna's real message? How could she tell them about his flag of death? "It's—it's kind of a long message," she said. "If I could have a glass of water, maybe sit down for a minute."

"Lucy." Her father's strong arm was about her. "We'll go inside."

It was Jim Bowie who recognized that Lucy had something important to say and that she was reluctant to speak in front of everyone. "Good idea," Bowie said. "Let's go inside. After this little lady has a minute to collect her thoughts, Will Travis will want to hear what she's got to say. 'Specially if she's got something important to tell him about Santa Anna."

"Come on, Lucy," William Bonner said, never taking his arm away from his daughter's shoulders. "I'm glad to see you, honey, but you took an awful chance riding so near the Mexican Army all by yourself."

"Yes, Pa," Lucy said dutifully, and when they walked into the old stone building she looked about and saw the straw pallets and blankets piled into the corners of the rooms, saw the big jugs of water, saw some of the ranchers she knew—saw everything and everybody but Jesse Lee Powell.

"You could've been taken prisoner," William Bonner was scolding, but scolding so lovingly that Lucy knew he wasn't really angry with her. "I want you to be more careful from now on Lucy. It's bad enough when Carlos acts the fool, but you—"

At the mention of Carlos's name, Lucy was reminded of her purpose in being there. "Where is Carlos? I have to bring him home with me. With you gone, Ma is so lonely. Pa, we *must* convince Carlos to come home."

William Bonner drank deeply of Lucy's deep dark eyes, so like her mother's. What he saw there convinced him that she was right. "Come," he said. "Let's go find him."

As they walked the length of the Alamo, Lucy found it hard to believe it was the same place she had left those weeks before. Then it had been like an elaborate campsite, a place where children played beneath the tables as their fathers cleaned rifles and their mothers roasted beef on spits. Now Fort Alamo was clearly a little city under a state of siege. Almost all of the women and children were gone. Guards watched at the walls, constantly checking the perimeter. Inside, the Alamo was in a state of watchful waiting. Men played solitaire, drank coffee, and waited for the Mexican Army to come crashing in.

In one corner, William and Lucy found Carlos playing a card game with some men. Lucy, seeing his little dark head bent over the cards, felt a wave of love. She didn't realize how much she had missed her little brother.

"Carlos," William Bonner said.

The boy turned toward his father's voice, saw Lucy, and knew why she was there. "I'm not goin' anywhere!" he said.

"Come, *querido*." William Bonner made excuses to Carlos's card companions and took his boy by the arm, off to a corner so they could have a talk man to man.

Lucy, watching discreetly, saw Carlos look over his shoulder to make sure that no one was watching. Then, wiping the tears from his eyes, he threw his arms around his father. Whatever had transpired between them, it was clear that William Bonner had convinced his young son that his place was at home.

William gave Lucy a little nod, and she knew she could approach their private corner now. "Oh, Carlos," she said, hugging her brother. "Ma needs you so much at home."

"I will come, Lucy, but only 'cause you and Ma

71

need me to take care of things. Otherwise, I'd never leave Pa."

William sighed. "I'm glad you're both going back," he said. "I don't want either of you around here when the fighting starts."

Lucy remembered the red flag and the size of the Mexican Army. Carlos would leave with her, they would ride to safety, but what about her father? And what about Jesse Lee?

"Pa," she started to ask her father. "Have you seen—"

But by then William Bonner had led them to the small room that Colonel Travis was using as his headquarters, and Lucy had no opportunity to ask her father about Jesse Lee.

"Look who rode in pretty as a picture," Jim Bowie said to William Travis. "Those Mexicans must be half-asleep."

Colonel Travis looked at Lucy's white face and the way she held onto her father's arm, and he quickly pulled out a chair for her. Quietly, he dismissed everyone except for Lucy, her father, and Jim Bowie from the room. "They weren't sleeping, were they, Lucy?" he asked.

Lucy shook her head and then told them about General Santa Anna and everything she had seen. She hadn't been able to count squadrons or battalions, but her description of the many soldiers bore out the information they had already had from the scouts.

It was when she came to the red flag that Lucy had

trouble speaking. Colonel Travis offered her a cup of water. She took a sip and tried to clear her throat. Finally, the words came out—the words about the general and his red flag of death.

"All right, Lucy," Colonel Travis said quietly. "You're a brave girl, and I guess we're all mighty proud of you. Will," he said, turning to her father. "Jim and I have got to talk."

William Bonner nodded, and he and Lucy left the two co-commanders of the Alamo alone.

"Lucy." William Bonner's voice was shaking. "When I think of you captured by those Mexicans! Anything could've happened."

"But nothing did, Pa." Now that she had fulfilled her obligations, it was time her heart had a turn. Lucy took her father's arm. "Pa," she said. "Have you seen—"

But before she could even say his name, they turned a corner, and he was there! Actually before her—Jesse Lee Powell—standing there.

Lucy let go of her father's arm and ran to him. He folded her in his arms and held her tightly to him. "Lucy," Jesse Lee said. "I couldn't believe it—couldn't believe it when I heard them say that Lucy Bonner had just ridden in."

"Lucy," William Bonner said, looking at his daughter in the young man's arms. "Lucy—"

"Oh, Pa, I'm sorry." Lucy broke free from Jesse Lee reluctantly. "You don't know Jesse Lee Powell."

"I know Jesse Lee," William Bonner said. "And I

know he stopped at our ranch, but I didn't know that *you* knew him quite so well."

"We met here at the barbecue, sir," Jesse Lee explained.

William Bonner kept his eyes on his daughter. "That doesn't seem quite long enough ago for you to be so friendly, does it now?"

Lucy blushed. "It's true, Pa. We haven't known each other very long, but—"

William Bonner shook his head and looked at the two young people sadly. "It's the war," he said. "If it weren't for the war the two of you wouldn't be rushing ahead quite so fast—"

"The war has nothing to do with it," Lucy interrupted.

"War or peace," Jesse Lee chimed in, "it would always be Lucy for me."

"If it weren't for the war," William Bonner said, "you wouldn't even have *met* Lucy."

"I can't believe that, sir," Jesse Lee said. "Somehow, some way, fate would have brought us together."

"And if it weren't for the war," William Bonner continued, "my daughter wouldn't be riding around the countryside by herself, wouldn't be throwing herself into a stranger's arms—"

"Jesse Lee is no stranger," Lucy said. She took her father's arm again. "Please try to understand, Pa. I love Jesse Lee as though I had known him all my life. Don't be angry."

William Bonner knew that for Lucy, who was usually so quiet about everything she felt, this was quite a statement. "I'm not angry, Lucy," her father said. "Only people do strange things when there's danger—things they may regret later on."

Jesse Lee spoke seriously to Mr. Bonner. "We won't do anything that we'll regret," he said. "I can promise you that, sir."

William Bonner looked at the tall young man. "I trust you, Jesse Lee, but I don't want Lucy hurt."

Before Jesse Lee could answer, Jim Bowie and William Travis came down the corridor.

"We're calling everybody together outside," Colonel Travis said. "We decided that everybody's got a right to hear Lucy's news."

"What news?" Jesse Lee asked.

"Outside," Colonel Travis said. "Tell everyone to gather around, Jesse Lee. You'll hear Lucy's news along with everyone else."

It was dusk when the men and women of the Alamo gathered around Lucy and the co-commanders of the fort. Someone had built a fire, and faces glimmered from the red flames.

"You better do the talking, Will," Jim Bowie said to Colonel Travis. "Reckon you're better at it than I am."

Not allowing himself to show much emotion, Colonel Travis told the people of the Alamo about General Santa Anna's ultimatum and about the grim promise of the red flag. There was silence. Then he told them about the large army that Lucy had seen and about the equipment the army carried with it. His words were greeted with silence once again.

No one spoke, no one moved, and William Travis went on. "We're hoping that Sam Houston will send help pretty soon. We're sending scouts to him, but we don't know when that help will come. Meanwhile, not me, nor Jim Bowie, will think less of anyone who wants to leave the Alamo right now." Silence greeted those words, too.

Finally, Jesse Lee spoke. "Seems as though Santy Anny has himself two flags, and we only got one!"

"We're flying the Lone Star flag of Texas," one of the men called out. "Ain't that good enough for you Tennessee boys?"

Jesse Lee threw his head back and laughed. "I'm so crazy about everything Texan that I want more—another flag—something to show Santy Anny what we think of his red flag. How about that? How about a flag with TEXAS written on it big?"

Everyone laughed. Lucy pulled off the large white silk square that she had worn knotted about her neck. "Could you use this, Jesse Lee?" she asked.

Jesse Lee's eyes sparkled as he took the scarf from Lucy's hands. He touched it to his lips before he passed it on to someone who offered to print TEXAS on the square of silk.

"You sure you know how to spell?" Lucy and Jesse Lee heard as they walked away from the firelight and into the surrounding darkness of the courtyard.

*   *   *

The two strolled around the side of the mission building and entered the small chapel that was now being used as a storeroom for food supplies.

Some of the chapel benches were still in place, and Lucy and Jesse Lee sat down on one of them. Jesse Lee put his arm around Lucy, and with a little sigh she let her head rest against his shoulder. "I'm so tired," Lucy said, closing her eyes. "Tired—but happy, too."

Jesse Lee bent to kiss her forehead. "Our kids are never going to believe us when we tell them about our courting days. Either I've been riding all night and I'm exhausted, or you've been riding all day and are all tuckered out."

"Kids?" Lucy stirred dreamily. "Are we going to have a whole lot of them?"

"Why sure," Jesse Lee said. "I come from a big family."

Children . . . the future . . . a wonderful future. Lucy sat up, suddenly wide awake. But with Santa Anna and his army, what guarantee was there that there would be any future for the two of them? What guarantee that they would ever have anything more than this one night?

She remembered how she had mocked Jesse Lee when he had talked about the short time they might have together, but now she was the one who wanted to say those words.

"Jesse Lee," she began, now knowing how to say exactly what she felt. "What if—what if—"

Jesse Lee's lips were tender against hers. "I told

you that night, Lucy, one kiss to seal our love. That's all I wanted then, and that's all I'll take from you now."

"But Jesse Lee—" Again, Lucy didn't know how to say the words, didn't know how to describe the yearning within her. But the wonderful thing was that with Jesse Lee she didn't need words. He knew how she felt because he felt the same way.

"I promised your pa," he said. "But even if I hadn't, this isn't the time, Lucy, you know that."

"I know," she admitted sadly. "But if anything happens to you, Jesse Lee—"

"Nothing's going to happen to me," he said, and stroked away the frown between her eyebrows. "I'm going to live forever because Lucy Bonner loves me!"

Suddenly he moved away from the bench and began capering around the chapel. "Lucy Bonner loves me!" he shouted. "Lucy Bonner loves me!"

"Jesse Lee," Lucy said, laughing in spite of herself. "Stop it!"

Jesse Lee came over to the bench and pulled Lucy to her feet and into his arms. "Am I telling the truth?" He kissed her eyes, the tip of her nose, and finally her lips. "Well, am I telling the truth or not? Does Lucy Bonner love me or doesn't she?"

Lucy put her arms around his neck. "Lucy Bonner loves you, Jesse Lee Powell." She raised her face for another kiss. "She loves you now—she'll love you tomorrow—she'll love you forever!"

Lucy's voice broke on that last word, and she buried her face against Jesse Lee's shoulder. *Forever.* What did the word *forever* mean when Santa Anna and his flag of death were waiting for Jesse Lee just a few short miles away?

Chapter 7

LUCY AND CARLOS LEFT THE ALAMO BEFORE DAWN
and rode side by side in silence. Lately there had been
too many goodbyes in her life, Lucy thought sadly.
She closed her eyes for a second to squeeze back the
tears as she remembered her father's warm hug in the
courtyard of the Alamo.

"Take care of your ma," he whispered. "Tell her I
love her. And take care of yourself, my darling Lucy."

When he said goodbye to his son, William Bonner
gave him a handshake, but then his son was in his
arms, too, and he held the boy close to him. "Take
care of your ma and Lucy," he said, trying his best to
sound cheerful. "You're the head man of the family,
Carlos, leastways until I get back."

Lucy was grateful that she and Jesse Lee had said a

private goodbye in the chapel storeroom. She didn't want anyone to share the sight of their last kiss.

Lucy and Carlos were about two miles from the Alamo when they heard it, the dull, thudding sound that made Lucy think of thunder. But the sky was clear, and the dawning sun promised a beautiful day.

"Lucy," Carlos asked his sister. "Did you hear that? What is it?"

Lucy patted her horse's neck. Blanca had shied at the unexpected noise and the tremor that she could feel in the ground. "Guns," Lucy said briefly. "Cannon. The Mexicans must be shelling the Alamo."

"How do you know?" Carlos said.

"I saw them," Lucy answered. "I saw the cannon. It can't be anything else."

"I'm going back," Carlos said, and he started to wheel his horse about.

"Carlos!" Lucy rode close and put her hands over his. "You can't. If I don't bring you back to the ranch, I don't know what'll happen to Ma. She's worried enough about Pa. You can't do this to her, Carlos."

Carlos sighed. "All right, Lucy, all right."

Lucy knew she was right when they rode up to the ranch, and her mother came out of the house to get a better view of the two riders. Once she realized that it was Lucy and Carlos, she didn't wait for them on the porch, but ran down the dirt road to greet them. "Lucy! Carlos!" Estrella Bonner was weeping. "Thank God you're all right."

Lucy and Carlos dismounted and walked with their mother between them to the house.

"Your father," Estrella asked. "How is your father?"

"He's all right, Ma," Lucy said. "Honest, he's all right."

"I wanted to stay with him," Carlos said. "And I should have. The moment I heard those guns I knew I should have."

"Guns?" Estrella said fearfully. "What guns?"

"Santa Anna's guns," Carlos said impatiently. "They're shelling the Alamo."

Estrella Bonner was crying again. "Oh, no!" she said. "Oh, no!"

"Carlos," Lucy said sharply. "They can shell the Alamo all they want, but the men inside are safe. Besides, Colonel Travis said that Sam Houston was sending help."

"But when?" Estrella asked. "When?"

When? Lucy knew that was the same question being asked at the Alamo. *When* was Sam Houston sending help? *When* would men from the Texas Volunteer Army get to the Alamo? *When* would volunteers from the United States get to the Alamo? No one knew, but not one of the men had chosen to leave the Alamo when Colonel Travis had given them the choice. Some of the men whose wives were still at the Alamo had pleaded with the women to leave, but a few had insisted on remaining at the fort.

I would have stayed with Jesse Lee, Lucy thought. *If he and I were married, I would have stayed right there with him.* And she admitted to herself that if it hadn't been for her parents, she would have stayed with Jesse Lee even though there had been no time for them to get married. But she also knew that Jesse Lee would never have let her stay.

"Get back safe to the ranch," he had said to her when they parted. "I want to think of my Lucy girl being safe. A man can't fight if he's worrying about the girl he loves."

Well, now she was safe, back home at the ranch. But what did that safety mean without Jesse Lee? Lucy looked at her mother and knew that she felt the same way. What good was safety if you weren't with the person you loved?

Day after day, the Bonners waited for some word from the Alamo. The two women and Carlos ran the ranch with the help of Ramiro's wife, his son Paco, and the *vaqueros* who remained.

"It's time to move the cattle to the north meadow," Carlos told Lucy and his mother.

"Isn't it too soon?" Estrella Bonner questioned.

"It's when Pa would have done it," Carlos answered, and the cattle were moved.

The three of them tried to do things the way William Bonner did them, and at night when they sat at the big dining table, the empty chair at the head of the table was a constant reminder of William Bonner's absence. Finally, Estrella set the table for the evening meal in the kitchen.

"This is much better, Ma," Lucy said with a sigh of relief. "That dining table—"

"It was too big," Carlos finished for her.

"Much too big," Lucy agreed.

"Too empty," Estrella said, "without your pa."

"How many days has it been, Lucy?" Carlos asked his sister the next day as the two of them tugged at the gate of a corral fence.

Lucy knew just what he meant. "It's been a week," she said. "It's been one whole week since we left the Alamo."

"It seems longer," Carlos said.

"I know," Lucy said. "I know."

Lucy took to crossing off the days on the calendar that hung in the pantry. So many days without her father, so many days without Jesse Lee. It was ten days, then eleven, twelve, and thirteen—and it was after the thirteenth day that two men rode up to the Bonner ranch bringing news.

They had been in San Antonio—not at the Alamo— but they had been close enough to know what happened. "They held Santa Anna off for thirteen days," one of the men said. "And with no help I figure that was a kind of a miracle."

"Yep, thirteen days," the other man said. "They held Santa Anna off for that long, but then, finally—"

Lucy looked at her mother. She didn't want to

question these men in front of her, but she had to know.

"Finally?" she asked.

"He took the fort," one of the men said. "Santa Anna did. Bowie and Travis couldn't hold out against all them guns and soldiers and cannon. We're on our way now to Sam Houston to tell him—" he stopped and looked warily at the Bonner family.

"To tell him—," Lucy prompted.

"To tell him that the Alamo is lost. And every man with it."

Estrella Bonner let out one piercing scream and then she was silent. It was Lucy who asked in a whisper, "Were there any wounded? Any prisoners?"

The man looked down at the ground. "No prisoners. He was flying the red flag, Santa Anna was. Oh, he let the women and children go—didn't touch them. But the men, he killed every last one of them. Travis, Bowie, Crockett—"

"Bonner," Lucy said, then added in a whisper, "Powell."

"Kin?" the man asked.

"Kin," Lucy answered.

The men got back on their horses and rode away. Estrella Bonner went quietly into the house, Carlos with her.

Lucy stayed outside for a minute and looked up at the darkening evening sky. The stars were just coming out, and Lucy stared at two of them that seemed to be shining more brightly than any of the others.

"Pa," she whispered. "Is that you up there? Are you a star now? Jesse Lee? Is that you? Are you a star with Pa?"

A cloud covered the two stars, and Lucy went into the house. She opened the door to the pantry and carefully drew a large black border around the date: March sixth, eighteen hundred and thirty-six. *The day the Alamo fell*, Lucy thought. *And the day my life ended. Oh, I'm still alive, all right, but my life—any real life that I might have had—is over.*

Jesse Lee, Jesse Lee, I'll never love anyone else, not ever again.

Lucy and Carlos were surprised at their mother's outward calm. They could hear her weeping when she was alone in the room she had shared so lovingly with William Bonner, but when she was with Lucy and Carlos she was composed.

It was two or three days after they had heard the news that Estrella became aware of what had happened to her daughter. "Lucy," she said. "For you, it's not just Pa, is it? That nice young man—Jesse Lee . . ."

Lucy hadn't cried until she heard her mother say his name, and then she repeated it with a wail. "Jesse Lee, Jesse Lee—"

Estrella Bonner took Lucy in her arms. "My poor Lucy," she said, rocking her the way she had when she was a baby. "My poor Lucy."

Lucy held onto her mother, and it was as though the

two of them were holding each other up. "You too, Ma, you too. I know what you're going through. Now I know."

Estrella shook her head. "You're young, Lucy, you're so young. In time—"

"Don't say anything, Ma," Lucy said, pulling away from her. "Please don't say anything. There will never be anyone else for me—never."

"All right, Lucy," her mother said. "All right. I understand. And now? What shall we do now?"

Lucy stood up straight. "We'll do what Pa would have wanted us to do, Ma. We'll run the ranch, the three of us. We'll manage. We'll do it for Pa."

"Yes," Estrella said in a small, sad voice. "It is what your father would have wanted. We won't give up. He didn't."

Carlos came into the room, and Lucy noticed how much older he looked. Bigger, somehow; taller, too, like a man. She reminded herself that he was almost fifteen and that he had done even more to take on the man's role in their family ever since they had heard the news about their father.

"What were you saying about Pa?" he asked.

"That we're going to keep on with the ranch," Estrella said, "just the way your father would have wanted us to do."

"I should have stayed with Pa," Carlos said unhappily. "I should never have left him."

"Carlos," Lucy said. "Pa wanted you to leave the Alamo—"

"Besides," Estrella interrupted, "what would we have done without you, Lucy and me? How would we have managed?"

"I should have stayed with Pa," Carlos repeated. "That's all I know. I should have stayed with Pa."

Chapter 8

LUCY, CARLOS, AND THEIR MOTHER WORKED ME-
chanically for the next few days, busy with their own
thoughts and sadness and each one determined to
wear a brave face for the sake of the others. They
would sit out the war between Mexico and Texas on
their ranch; there didn't seem to be anything else they
could do.

But a tired man on a lathered pinto horse changed
their minds. Lucy saw him first, riding fast on the road
that led up to the ranch house, and for a minute her
heart pounded with anticipation—from a distance the
man looked like Jesse Lee. But as he drew closer she
reminded herself that it couldn't be Jesse Lee, not
ever. Jesse Lee would never ride up to the ranch
again.

The man was a stranger, and Lucy's tiny spurt of

happiness changed to one of fear. The last time a stranger had ridden up to the ranch it was with the tragic news about the Alamo. What was this man going to tell them now?

She was right to feel afraid, she realized, after he gave her his short message as quickly as he could.

"Sam Houston sent me," he said. "I'm with the Texas Volunteer Army. He wants all you folks around here to move on. Santa Anna and his army are heading this way, and Houston doesn't have enough men to protect you."

"Move on?" Lucy asked indignantly. "But this is our ranch, our home. How can we move on?"

"You can die on a ranch just as good as at any other place," the man said. He looked around. "Who's running this ranch?"

"There's me, my mother, and my brother," Lucy said, "and the hands."

"Two women and one man," the messenger said, shaking his head. "How old's your brother?"

"Just about fifteen."

"Two women and a *boy*. You better not even think of staying around here."

Carlos and Estrella had come out of the house to join Lucy, and Carlos was angry at the soldier's words. "I'm not a boy," he said. "I'm a man. Tell me, does Sam Houston need more volunteers?"

"Sure he does," the soldier said. "There's bound to be a showdown with Santa Anna sometime soon."

"Then I'm coming with you," Carlos said. "I'm joining Sam Houston's army."

"Carlos," Estrella Bonner said. "You can't."

Carlos turned to his mother. "I got to, Ma, don't you see? I'll never forgive myself if I don't. I got to make it up to Pa, about leaving him at the Alamo."

"You folks lose someone at the Alamo?" the soldier asked.

"My husband," Estrells Bonner said.

"And the man I was going to marry," Lucy added.

The soldier shook his head and then turned to Carlos. "You better saddle up, son, if you're coming with me."

"My name is Carlos Bonner," Lucy's brother said. "It won't take me long. I'll ride with you."

Carlos went into the house on the run, and minutes later he was outside once again, heading for the barn.

Estrella and Lucy looked at each other. They both knew there was no use trying to argue with Carlos. Lucy looked worriedly at her mother, but since the terrible news from the Alamo Estrella had become both resigned and stronger.

"I don't blame him," Estrella said to Lucy. "I just wish I could join the army, too."

Lucy put her arm around her mother's shoulders. "It isn't just Carlos who's leaving, Ma. We've got to leave, too."

"But how can we, Lucy? Two women alone."

"You won't exactly be alone, ma'am," the soldier said. "I've warned a lot of folks around here that the Mexicans are headed this way."

He turned to Lucy. "Sam Houston says you'd best be moving east and then south. To Washington-on-the-Brazos, that's where he's heading. Maybe you can team up with your nearest neighbors. Two wagons traveling together might be safer than one."

"The Shumanns," Lucy said. "We can travel with the Shumanns." But even as she said it, Lucy wondered what it would be like traveling in the company of Dirk Shumann. But this was an emergency. She'd have to put her personal likes and dislikes aside.

The hardest moment of the day was saying goodbye to Carlos. Lucy was surprised that her mother didn't try to stop her brother from leaving, but with the death of William Bonner, Estrella had taken on a fatalistic view of life.

"I'll be back, Ma," Carlos said, hugging his mother. "After the war is over I'll come right back to the ranch. But will you and Lucy be all right?"

"We'll manage just fine," Lucy assured him, understanding that her brother's need to join the fighting was greater than her need to have him stay with them.

Carlos looked relieved. He wanted to join Sam Houston's army, but it was clear that he also wanted to get away from the sad and depressing place that their ranch had become.

Lucy and her mother remained on the road in front of the ranch, staring after Carlos until their eyes ached and they could no longer see any dust from his horse's hooves.

"I'll ride over to the Shumann's, Ma," Lucy said, "and see how long it'll take them to get ready to leave. I guess we should be starting out tomorrow at sunup.

"Why don't you tell Paco to get the big wagon ready for us? And see if any of the hands want to come with us.

"Tell Greta Shumann to pack plenty of warm things," Estrella said, as sure as Lucy was that the Shumanns would want to leave with them. "We may be away from home for a long time."

Lucy rode off to the Shumann ranch. The war had changed her mother, she realized. It had given her more strength than she had ever had. And Lucy knew that it had done the same for her. What had happened to the shy girl who hated to talk to strangers, who could barely talk to boys? She was nowhere around when Lucy had to face those men of the Mexican Army. She wasn't there when Lucy fell in love with Jesse Lee. She was glad to say goodbye to the shy Lucy, and she understood something her father had told her a long time before. "Danger brings out a man's courage," was the way he had put it. *And a woman's, too,* Lucy thought.

What she wasn't prepared for was the reception she received from the Shumanns.

"Leave? Why should we leave?" Johann Shumann was angry at the very suggestion. "We came here from

Pennsylvania to farm and ranch, nothing more. Who cares if Texas belongs to the Mexicans? What has that got to do with running a ranch?"

"But Sam Houston sent a warning," Lucy persisted. "He said that the Mexican Army was headed this way and we might be in danger if we didn't leave."

"You, maybe," Mr. Shumann said with a sneering kind of pity, "but not us. We didn't have anyone fighting at the Alamo. We're neutral."

"My father died at the Alamo," Lucy said angrily, "and so did many others."

"I'm sorry about that," Johann Shumann said, "but that has nothing to do with us. And Will Bonner would have been a lot smarter to stay at home where he belonged."

At that, Lucy clicked a command to Blanca and was riding away when she heard Mrs. Shumann say, "Johann, you should not have said that."

Lucy was so furious that she moved Blanca into a gallop, and it was some minutes later that she heard another horseman come pounding up behind her.

"Lucy!" she heard Dirk shout. "Wait!"

Lucy slowed Blanca down. Maybe Mrs. Shumann had persuaded Mr. Shumann to leave their ranch, but she didn't care anymore. She didn't want to combine wagons with the Shumanns, not after hearing what Johann Shumann had to say.

"It's too late," she said when Dirk came riding up beside her. "You and your family will just have to make it on your own, Dirk. My mother and I won't travel with you."

"Travel with us?" Dirk asked. "Didn't you hear my father? We're not leaving our ranch."

"Then why did you come after me?"

"I thought by now you might be ready to listen to some sense, Lucy. You and your mother don't have to leave either. The two of you can come and stay at our house until the danger is over. The Mexicans won't harm you if you're with us. After all, we never fought against them."

Lucy looked at him with disgust. "Well, thank you," she said, hoping that he heard the sarcasm in her voice.

But Dirk was impervious to Lucy's subtle barbs. "That's all right," he said. "It's the right thing to do for our nearest neighbors, especially since we'll be joining our ranches together some time soon."

"What?" Lucy looked at him with rage. "What are you talking about?"

Dirk shrugged. "I know your man is dead, Lucy. And maybe you even went a little too far with him, but that's all right. Now it's just you and me. And after the Mexicans win, when the war is over, we can get married and the Shumann-Bonner spread can become one of the biggest ranches in Texas."

Lucy glared at him. "You—you smug, stupid fool," she said. "I'll *never* marry you. I hate you, Dirk Shumann, and just talking to you betrays everything that my father and Jesse Lee Powell fought and died for."

Dirk wasn't used to this new, angry Lucy. He glared back at her as a flush covered his face. "Jesse Lee Powell, Jesse Lee Powell," Dirk sneered. "Where is he now? Where is he when you need a man to take care of you?"

Lucy was too upset to speak. The words she wanted to say were stuck in her throat, and all she wanted to do was get away from him.

She put her heels to Blanca's flanks and galloped away from Dirk. If only she could ride faster still, fast enough to get away from those terrible words. *Where is he when you need a man to take care of you?* Oh, where are you, Jesse Lee, where are you? She was crying so hard she couldn't even see the road, but it didn't matter because Blanca knew the way back to the ranch. Luckily, Dirk had stopped following her, but his poisonous words would stay with her for a long time to come.

By the time Lucy got back to the ranch, the wind had dried her tears, but Estrella could tell by the look on her daughter's face that there had been trouble with the Shumanns. "Never mind, Lucy," she said, not wanting to know the details. "We'll be all right without the Shumanns."

"We'll have to be," Lucy said. "Do any of the men from the ranch want to come with us?"

"No," Estrella said. "They think they'll be all right

in their own homes. They said they'll try to take care of the ranch for us—if Santa Anna lets them."

Lucy nodded. She understood the ranch hands and the *vaqueros*. Most of them were born across the Rio Grande and believed that they could deal with the Mexican Army. They'd offer them a few steers and hope that Santa Anna was only out to conquer those who had dared fight against him.

By first light the next morning, Lucy and her mother left the ranch, their wagon filled with whatever clothing and household goods they thought they might need. The wagon was pulled by a team of four horses, and Lucy had Blanca attached with a loose rein to the back of the wagon.

"Lucy," and there was just a touch of the old tremulousness in Estrella Bonner's voice, "do you have any idea which way we're heading? Maybe we should just stay on the ranch."

"We'll head toward Washington-on-the-Brazos," Lucy said with a confidence that she didn't feel. "That's where we'll find Sam Houston and the Texas Volunteer Army. We'll be safe enough once we're there."

"But *until* we get there," Estrella said. "What about *until* we get there?"

"Nothing's going to happen to us, Ma," Lucy said. "We'll be fine." But all the same, she was glad she had loaded one of her father's pistols and put it under a blanket in the wagon. There was a shotgun there, too, and even though Lucy had never shot to kill anything in her whole life, she felt that the guns would be good for something. She didn't think she could actually shoot anyone, but maybe just pointing a gun would be enough. She certainly hoped so.

Chapter 9

LUCY AND ESTRELLA WERE PART OF A CARAVAN OF wagons all trying to move out of the way of the advancing Mexican Army. Lucy and her mother didn't know any of the people in the other wagons, who had come from remote farms and ranches. No one asked the Bonner women to join up with them, which surprised Lucy, although Estrella understood it.

"Two women alone," she explained to her daughter. "They think we'll be a burden."

"I'd never let us be a burden to anyone," Lucy said indignantly.

"I know that," Estrella said. "But they don't. Besides, none of these people seem to have a clear idea of where they're headed."

That was certainly true, Lucy agreed. Some days she recognized the same wagons traveling either behind or in front of them. But then a wagon driver would get a new idea and turn off to another road.

"Better go this way, miss," one man, kinder than most, suggested to Lucy as he whipped his wagon past the Bonners heading toward a crossroad in their path. "You take that road, you're bound to run into Santa Anna."

"How do you know that?" Lucy asked.

The man shook his head. "Don't know for sure, but that's what I heard."

There were as many rumors flying about the Texas roads as there were people traveling on them, but Lucy stuck to her original plan to reach Washington-on-the-Brazos.

"Are you sure that's the right way to go?" Estrella asked.

"I'm not sure, Ma," Lucy admitted, "but I want us to light somewhere. Most of these folks are going around in circles."

Estrella sighed. Days sitting up on a hard wagon seat, nights camped in the open next to a small fire preparing a small amount of meat in a black iron skillet over the same fire—she was close to exhausted, and she didn't think Lucy felt much better.

Estrella smiled as she looked at her daughter. Lucy looked so serious as she poked at a piece of steak sizzling in a skillet. William used to take Lucy with him when he had to go to a far corner of the ranch, and the things he had taught her stood them in good stead now. It was clear, though, that one thing he had never taught her was how to cook out in the open. Estrella knew that the steak would be charred black on the outside and raw and cold on the inside. She did her best to eat something, though, after Lucy put a piece of meat on her plate.

"I don't understand it," Lucy said, staring at the unappetizing food. "When Ramiro cooked barbecue it never looked like this."

That made Estrella laugh. "Lucy, Ramiro spent a whole day on his *barbacoa*—two days, really, when you remember how long it took him to make a sauce— his precious *salsa*."

"*Salsa*," someone echoed. The Bonner women had camped beside the Brazos River with a clump of cottonwood trees behind them, and now they heard a voice, speaking softly in Spanish, coming from behind the trees. "It is good to hear talk of *salsa*. It makes me think of home."

Lucy jumped up, angry with her self for leaving the guns in the wagon on the far side of the cottonwoods.

There was a rustling sound, and soon a Mexican soldier emerged from the trees, followed by another soldier, and another, and still another. The first sol- dier—the one who had spoken—approached the small fire and looked down into the skillet. He was clearly disappointed.

"But you spoke of *salsa*," he said. "There is no *salsa*. And that"—he pointed his drawn pistol at the meat that still remained in the skillet—"that is not even a proper *barbacoa*."

Lucy took a deep, gasping breath. She had been so sure that they were headed toward Sam Houston and safety, but now they seemed to have crossed the path of the Mexican Army!

For a moment, neither Estrella nor Lucy spoke, and then Lucy answered in Spanish. "We have no *salsa* and no *barbacoa*, either. We are homeless and have nothing, so please leave us alone."

The soldier came closer and looked at her. "You speak perfect Spanish. Are you a Mexican?"

Say yes, one part of Lucy's mind advised her. *Say yes, and they will go away and leave you alone.* But the memory of her father and Jesse Lee Powell was too strong. "I am a Texan," she said, "from San Antonio."

The soldier shrugged. "A Texan," he said. "What is a Texan? There is no such thing. Texas is part of Mexico."

Again, sensible, practical Lucy advised her not to respond, but the other Lucy—the daughter of the man who had died at the Alamo and the girl who loved Jesse Lee—that Lucy couldn't be practical. "Texas won't be part of Mexico for long," she blurted out. "One day Texas will be free!"

To Lucy's suprise the soldier didn't get angry. Instead he laughed. He reminded Lucy of the Mexican lieutenant who had stopped her that day when she rode to the Alamo. "Too bad you're not on our side, *señorita*," he said. "You're a very bold young woman."

Lucy forced herself to smile. She didn't want the soldier to know that for all her brave words she felt a great deal of fear, but the pride she felt for her father and Jesse Lee made her hide that fear.

Estrella stared at her daughter. She was no longer shy little Lucy. *She has her father's courage*, Estrella thought. *But now we have had enough conversation with the enemy.* "My daughter told you the truth, *señor* soldier. We have nothing—we can give you nothing. Please leave us alone."

The soldier looked at the contents of the black skillet once again. "You have no food worth eating, that is clear. But you do have horses." He whistled, and one of his men led a prancing Blanca into the firelight.

"Blanca!" Lucy called out. "No!"

"And that's not all, Sergeant," the man who held Lucy's prize horse said. "There are four others back there."

"No!" Lucy ran past the sergeant and tried to pull Blanca's reins out of the soldier's hands. "You can't have our horses. Blanca has been mine since she was a foal. My father gave her to me. And we need the others to pull the wagon."

"We need them, too, *señorita*," the sergeant said shortly, "to pull our cannon across the river."

"You can't take my horses," Lucy shouted, struggling to get Blanca away from the soldier. "You can't!"

The sergeant held Lucy back. "This is war, *señorita*," he told her. "We must take what we can get—and we need your horses."

"*We* need our horses," Lucy said furiously. "And if you take them, I—I'll—"her anger prevented her from saying more.

"You'll do what, *señorita?*" the sergeant asked, grinning. "Two women? There is nothing you can do."

"Just let me get to my wagon," Lucy said, beyond all reason. "And then you'll see what I can do!"

The men laughed at the beautiful young girl. Anger had made her more beautiful still. Her dark hair had come loose about her shoulders, and her high cheekbones were flushed scarlet.

"Enough, Lucy," Estrella said sharply. "Let them take the horses, and let them go."

"Mama," Lucy said, anguish taking her back to her childhood days when she had called Estrella *Mama* not the abbreviated *Ma*. "Mama, I can't give up Blanca—I won't! Pa gave me Blanca."

"Blanca doesn't matter now," Estrella said, more aware than Lucy of the danger they were in. "We can manage without Blanca."

"And the other horses?" Lucy asked. "Without horses we're trapped."

She looked at her mother, her look saying as clearly

as words: *I know we're in danger, but we can't just give in.*

Lucy heard the sound of a rider coming from the direction of the wagon. Somebody from the Texas Volunteer Army, she thought prayerfully, someone to save them from these men who would steal their horses!

She sagged with disappointment when she saw that the rider was another Mexican. This one, from the look of his gold-buttoned and gold-braided uniform, was an officer.

"Sánchez," the officer said sharply to the sergeant who was still holding Lucy away from Blanca. "What is all this?"

The sergeant released Lucy and saluted the officer. "Horses, Captain Seguín, we've found horses."

"Looks like you've found more than horses," the captain replied. "The general's orders are that no women or children are to be hurt."

"I haven't hurt anyone." The sergeant sounded aggrieved. "Or I wouldn't have. But this one"—he indicated Lucy—"she's a wildcat."

"These men are trying to steal our horses, Captain—Captain—" Lucy paused, recognizing the familiar name. "Did he say Captain *Seguín?*"

The captain saluted her. "Captain José Seguín, *señorita*. I'm sorry if my men have troubled you."

"But *Seguín*. We have a friend—his name is Juan Seguín."

Estrella stood beside her daughter. "Yes, Juan. Don Erasmo Seguin's son—from San Antonio."

The captain looked somber. "That is one of the tragedies of this war. Juan Seguin—I have never met him, but I know from my father that we have relatives in Texas, and I am sure that Juan Seguin is one of them. *Qué lástima*—what a pity—cousin fighting against cousin."

"A pity, yes," Lucy said, her voice hoarse with tears that she was holding back. "Because Juan Seguin was at the Alamo, too."

"Ah, so he died there. That is sad news," Captain José Seguin said. Then he realized that Lucy had said Seguin was at the Alamo *too,* and it made him ask, "You had someone special at the Alamo, *señorita?"*

"Yes," Lucy said, finding it unbearable to say more.

"I am sorry," the captain said quietly. "I know about the Alamo."

"And you?" Lucy asked sharply. "Were you at the Alamo, Captain?"

He shook his head. "No," he said, sounding relieved. "I was not at the Alamo. My regiment came across the Rio Grande after the battle."

Lucy looked at the tall, dark-haired captain. There was something about him—even though he was the enemy—that reminded her of Juan Seguin.

"You look like him," she said at last.

"Like who?"

"Like Juan Seguin," Estrella supplied. "Yes, I see it, too. You look quite a lot like Juan."

The captain looked at the two women and then signaled to the sergeant who was still holding Blanca's reins. "Sergeant, what are you doing with that horse?"

"I was requisitioning it, sir. The army needs horses badly."

"Is this your horse, *señorita?*" the captain asked Lucy.

She nodded, and despite herself her dark eyes filled with tears. "Yes. Her name is Blanca. My father gave her to me."

The captain saw the tears and saw how desperately Lucy was fighting for self-control. He knew, without her having to tell him, that her father was one of the men killed at the Alamo. "I think the army can manage with one less horse, Sergeant. Take Blanca, *señorita.*"

Lucy ran to the horse, took the reins, and put her arm around Blanca's neck, trying to soothe the nervous animal.

"All right," the sergeant said with disgust. "Then we'll just take the other four."

"But, Captain," Lucy said, walking over to José Seguin, Blanca trailing after her, "How can we get our wagon across the Brazos without our horses? We need them. My mother and I must get to some town where we'll be safe."

The captain looked at her somberly. "I don't know if there is such a place in Texas," he said.

"Captain," the sergeant argued. "We need those

four horses. We have cannon to get across the river and not enough horses to do the job."

"Then get them from the ranches around here," the captain said angrily. "We've passed ranches with horses—and men. Get the horses from them, Sergeant, not from two women who are trying to escape the war."

The sergeant shook his head, but there was nothing more he could say after the officer had given his command.

Captain Seguin wanted to do more for Lucy and Estrella. "Can you manage to get across the Brazos without help, *señorita*? I can have my men hitch the horses to your wagon and help you cross the river."

Lucy was so tired that she yearned to say yes, yearned to accept the captain's offer, and she knew that no one would blame her if she did. But he was the enemy. He didn't look like the enemy, he didn't sound like the enemy, but it was his army that had killed her father and Jesse Lee. "Thank you, Captain Seguin," she said, "but we'll manage. My mother and I have come this far without help, and we'll get to Washington-on-the-Brazos all right."

"Washington-on-the-Brazos," the captain said, shaking his head, and Lucy felt that he would have liked to say more, give her some warning, perhaps. But if she thought of him as the enemy, he had to see her the same way, and that made him powerless to give her more information.

"Sergeant," Captain José Seguin ordered. "Mount

up and take your men back to the road. We passed a ranch with a large *hacienda* and barns a few miles back. You'll find horses there."

The captain waited until his men had ridden off, and then he said to Lucy, "We meet at a bad time, *señorita*. It's too bad I never came to Texas before the war."

Lucy met the captain's eyes and saw that he was complimenting her. The new Lucy she kept discovering every day helped her find a way to answer him. "Texas was very different before the war," she said. "We were all very different. Especially me."

The captain tipped his hat to her and mounted his horse. *"Señora,"* he said, saluting Estrella Bonner. *"Señorita,* I hope I have not disgraced the name of Seguin in your eyes."

Estrella answered, "If—if ever this war is over, I shall tell Don Erasmo Seguin of what you have done for us, Captain."

"If ever this war is over," the captain echoed sadly. "Yes, let us hope that time comes very soon." His last wordless salute went to Lucy before he turned and rode off into the darkness.

"If ever this war is over," Estrella said once again. "If ever . . ."

Estrella's voice trailed off as Lucy hitched Blanca to a cottonwood close to the small fire that was becoming a mass of smoldering ashes. She threw a few more broken tree branches on the fire and watched them catch and flame.

Lucy wished she had more wood, enough to make a great, blazing bonfire. She hated the dark, she realized, as she looked at the blackness just a few yards away. She had never been afraid of the dark before, but she was afraid of it now. You never know what can come out of the dark to attack you, she thought. You never know.

Chapter 10

LUCY HAD REFUSED CAPTAIN SEGUIN'S HELP IN crossing the Brazos River, but now she wondered if she shouldn't have accepted it. She had become adept at hitching the horses to the wagon, but she had no idea how to lead them into the river and across.

It seemed simple enough. She told her mother to sit on the wagon seat. Then she urged the two lead horses into the water. But the horses were skittish. They had been trained to work on the Bonner ranch, where crossing rivers was not part of any duties ever taught them by William Bonner.

"We'll have to camp on this side of the river for a while," Lucy told her mother. "Maybe some other folks'll come along and give us a hand."

"I hope so," Estrella said wearily. "I'd like to stop living out of this wagon. Do you think Washington-on-the-Brazos has a hotel? Or maybe even a rooming house where we could stop?"

"I'm sure it has," Lucy said. "And even if it's nothing fancy, at least we'll be safe with Sam Houston and his men there."

The two women sat down by the river bank, and, just as Lucy had predicted, by early afternoon a wagon carrying a large family pulled up beside theirs.

A tobacco-chewing man, sitting on the front seat of his wagon, looked over at Estrella and Lucy. "You folks planning to cross the Brazos?" he asked.

"We'd like to," Lucy answered. "But we could use a little help."

"Could you now? Well, where's your menfolk?"

"Dead and in the Army," Lucy said, feeling the words like so many hard stones touching her heart. "My father is dead, and my brother's a volunteer in the Texas Army."

"Well, that's mighty curious." The man turned his head sideways and spit out a stream of dark brown tobacco juice. "They didn't show much sense, did they? Leaving their women to fend for themselves."

"We've done all right so far," Lucy said, bristling.

"So far," the man smirked. "Well, what about right now, sis? You don't seem to be doing just fine right now, do you?"

Lucy looked at her mother, and the two of them understood each other so completely that they didn't say a word. They simply sat down in a very leisurely fashion back on the river bank once more. "We're planning to camp here for a few days," Lucy said. "It's kind of peaceful, and we're in no real hurry to cross the Brazos."

The man grunted. "I thought you said you were in need of some help in crossing—that's what you said."

"Oh sure," Lucy said. "I said that, all right. We will need a little help a few days from now, when we decide we want to cross the river."

The man looked at her as though he didn't believe one word she had said. His gaze shifted to Blanca, who was quietly chewing a mouthful of dandelions.

"Well, now," he said craftily. "Happens that if you want to cross now, I could maybe give you a hand."

"That's very kind of you," Lucy said, surprised at his offer.

"And maybe you could do a little something for me," the man continued. "That there white horse sure is a pretty little thing. I figure maybe we could trade. I'll give you a hand across the Brazos, and you give me that white horse."

Lucy got to her feet. "No one is taking Blanca," she said, doing her best to keep calm. "I managed to keep her from some Mexican soldiers last night, and I guess I can manage to keep her from you."

The man heard the words *Mexican soldiers* and was quick to apply the reins across the backs of his horses. "Mex soldiers over this far? We heard they were way south o'here. Sam Houston's men said they were nowhere around here. We better get moving. Sorry, sis, can't pass the time of day with you anymore—we got to move on!''

And at his command his horses moved into the Brazos River and started their wet trip across. Lucy watched as the man handed the reins to his wife, jumped into the water, and waded over to his lead horses. With shouts and tugs he urged his team across the river.

"So much for his offer to give us a hand," Lucy said. "Not that I would have given him Blanca anyway."

"I don't want to give up Blanca, either," Estrella said, looking at the team of horses as it struggled up the opposite bank. "But Lucy, we can't get across the Brazos without help—that much is clear."

"We'll wait, Ma," Lucy said. "Someone else is bound to come along, someone who'll help us without taking Blanca."

But even though they had camped at the narrowest point of the Brazos—the best spot to cross the river, Lucy thought—hours went by without any other wagon appearing.

"It's because people are going in so many different directions," Estrella Bonner said, getting ready for another night on the hard ground beside their small campfire. "You heard that man—no one seems to know from which direction the Mexican Army is coming. Lucy, do you think we should go back to our ranch?"

"Go back to what, Ma? Sam Houston sent word for us to get out of there. How can we go back?"

Estrella balanced an enamel pot of coffee on a network of twigs and branches above the fire. If the food they had was hardly edible, at least they had strong black coffee to keep them going.

"But Lucy," Estrella said, ever so softly. "Are you sure that Sam Houston knows what he's doing? Maybe he's wrong, too. You heard that man—he said that Sam Houston's men told him there were no Mexican soldiers this far north."

Lucy was worried. The same thought had occurred to her. She shook her head and frowned. She suddenly felt very young. She felt like the Lucy she had been before the tragedy of the Alamo. Her father was right when he said the war changes people, makes everyone move fast, too fast. The old Lucy would never have had to handle so much responsibility, and the new Lucy wished that she didn't have to, either. "Oh, Ma," Lucy said, close to tears. "I just don't know!"

Estrella sat down and put both arms around her. "Never mind, my Lucy, we're doing just fine, we really are." She kissed her daughter's brow. "Your father would be proud of you. So would Jesse Lee."

Jesse Lee. Hearing his name put Lucy right over the edge. She was so tired, so very tired. She had been dealing with everything—packing the wagon, driving it, hitching and unhitching the horses, not letting the sergeant take her beloved Blanca, handling that terrible tobacco-chewing man. But suddenly it was all too much, especially when she realized how different everything would be if she had Jesse Lee by her side. "Oh, Ma!" Lucy cried, burying her head in her hands. "How can you stand it? How can you? Teach me how. You and Pa—you loved each other so much—how can you go on without him? How can I go on without Jesse Lee?"

Estrella's arm was about Lucy's bowed shoulders. *I can go on because I have you,* she thought, but she didn't say those words because she knew they would be no help to her daughter. *And you must go on because you're so young—so young—and there will be other good days for you.* But she didn't say that either, because she knew that Lucy would deny the possibility that there would ever be another man in her life—someone who wasn't Jesse Lee.

All Estrella Bonner could say was, "We must go on, Lucy. Your father would have wanted us to. He would have expected it. We can't let him down." She gave her daughter a little hug. "You're tired, Lucy. Things will look better tomorrow—you'll see."

Lucy sat up straight once again. "I'm sorry, Ma," she whispered. "I didn't mean to—"

"You didn't," Estrella reassured her with a smile. "You're a wonder, Lucy. You can do anything. Except when it comes to *barbacoa*, of course. Maybe I should cook tonight."

Lucy smiled through her tears and built up the fire again as her mother sliced beef and began to pile it into the sizzling-hot black skillet.

"If we only had an onion," Estrella said as she looked at the cooking meat. "This might not be so bad with an onion."

"Ah." A voice came to them from behind the cottonwood trees. "And I was just thinking if I only had some meat to go with my poor onion. I'd be a happy man."

"The Mexicans!" Lucy exclaimed. She jumped up, remembering the soldiers who had appeared the night before. "They're back. But this time I'm ready." She picked up her father's pistol and aimed it at the dark patch of trees. "Come on out of there!" she shouted. "Come on out or I'll shoot!" And she wondered what she would do if she actually had to shoot.

"Please, please!" A short plump man, who looked even more plump because of his brightly colored green and white checked jacket, emerged from the trees. "Don't shoot, anything but that," he said. "I'd rather eat my onion without the meat—anything's better than being shot!"

Lucy lowered the pistol and looked at the man as though he had appeared from some strange dream. "Who are you?" she asked, while her mother stared. "What are you doing here?"

"What am I doing here?" the man repeated cheerfully. "I've been asking myself that for days. As for who I am—and with a flourish he reached into his vest

pocket and brought out a slightly dirty white card—
"this is who I am."

Estrella took the card, and Lucy read over her
shoulder, "Patrick James O'Houlihan."

"That's me," the man said with a smile and a bow to
Lucy and Estrella.

"But Mister O'Hou—O'Houlihan—"

"Ah, Patrick, please."

"Patrick, then," Lucy said. "What are you doing
here?"

Patrick James O'Houlihan shook his head. "I have a
bad sense of direction, that's my main trouble. I'm a
peddler, ma'am—needles, threads, knives, some ex-
cellent cough medicine—anything that anyone might
be needing when they live far from a town or city. I
carry it in my wagon. I was a peddler for many years in
the state of Louisiana when I decided to try the
territory of Texas. I must say"—he shook his head—
"business is not as good here as it was in Louisiana—
houses are too far apart—but I was getting along until
a day or two ago when I guess I should have turned
right instead of turning left, and I ran into this big
bunch of soldier fellers—"

"Was it the Mexican Army?" Lucy asked.

"I suppose so," Patrick O'Houlihan said. "I tried to
tell them that I had no fight with them, me being from
Louisiana—and from Ireland before that—but they
weren't inclined to listen. Besides, I couldn't understand them, they talked in that foreign jabber, and they
seemed to have a bit of trouble understanding me."

"Mister—I mean, Patrick," Lucy said. "There's a war on."

"Ah, don't I know that now," the man said sadly. "Those men took everything from my wagon, all my supplies—they seemed to like my cough medicine especially—and they left me with next to nothing. Very little food, and almost nothing to peddle. Ah, well, I guess I should be grateful they left me my wagon and my horse—and my life."

"You're welcome to stay by our fire," Estrella said, "and to share our *barbacoa*, such as it is. I am Estrella Bonner, and this is my daughter Lucy."

Estrella and Lucy were each offered a bow once again, along with a handshake. The little man brightened when he looked down at the contents of the iron skillet. "Beefsteak, is it? That's a wonder, for sure. I haven't tasted meat for days. Now, ladies, if I may contribute my onion to the party, we'll have a feast!"

Estrella smiled. "Hardly a feast," she said.

"Perhaps you'd let me give you ladies a hand," Patrick O'Houlihan offered. "I've been doing my own cooking on the open road for years, and I'm not bad at it, if I do say so myself, even though I shouldn't."

Estrella and Lucy were grateful to give up the chore of cooking to the peddler, who ran to his small covered wagon and brought forth an assortment of boxes and tins. It seemed that the Mexicans hadn't taken all his supplies after all.

The Bonner women watched with fascination as Patrick added a pinch of this and a spoonful of that to the skillet. He murmured and hummed as he stirred. "A bit of salt, some pepper, mmm, yes, dried mushrooms, and my fine onion, sliced. And my tomato! To be sure—my tomato."

After he finished stirring, he found an old pot cover in the back of his wagon and covered the skillet. He then sat down on the ground, his back against a tree, and beamed. "An hour or so," he said, "and it will be fit to eat for anyone, even for one of the lost kings of Ireland, God rest their souls!"

Estrella and Lucy exchanged glances and smiled— actually smiled for the first time in a long, long time. Then Lucy gave a little laugh, and Estrella joined in. The peddler looked on in amazement as the two women hugged each other and laughed.

"It's been so long," Estrella said, wiping her eyes, caught somewhere between laughter and tears.

"Too long," Lucy agreed. "Far too long."

"What is it?" Patrick O'Houlihan asked, looking at them worriedly. "I hope I've done nothing to offend?"

"Not at all," Lucy said, trying to explain. "It's just been so long since we've talked to anyone—met anyone—who's been able to take our minds off the war. Mister O'—"

"Patrick."

"Patrick—your coming along just at this moment— it's a miracle!"

"A miracle for me, too, meeting you fine ladies. I'm used to traveling by myself, but it's a different matter altogether when you get caught up in the middle of a war. Perhaps," he said, lifting the lid from the skillet and giving a judicious sniff, "perhaps—if you wouldn't think it too forward of me—we could team up and be traveling out of harm's way together?"

"That would be wonderful," Estrella said.

"We'd welcome it," Lucy added. "And maybe together we would figure out a way to cross the Brazos."

"I'm sure we can," Patrick James O'Houlihan said. "I've crossed wider and deeper rivers than this. We'll look into the matter in the morning, if you will. But tonight—tonight you'll try my Irish New Orleans Stew."

"Irish New Orleans Stew," and that made Estrella smile again.

"Plates," Lucy said. "I'm afraid we only have two plates."

"No, no," Patrick said. "You leave all that to me."

He ran to his wagon again and brought back three plates, each decorated with a border of pink rosebuds. "Those Mexican fellers didn't take my china plates. Apparently, they didn't like the pattern."

Patrick O'Houlihan served helpings of stew to Lucy and her mother, and then he stood back, frowning slightly, waiting for them to taste and comment.

"Oh, this is wonderful," Lucy said, feeling hungry for the first time in days.

"Marvelous," Estrella said between bites. "Even better than Ramiro's." Thoughts of the old ranch hand made Estrella feel wistful for a moment, but Patrick's good humor kept the mood light.

The plump Irishman beamed, "Well, then, I think I'll just try a bit myself."

He served himself, ate, and said, "Not bad, not too bad. Maybe if I had put in more salt—"

"No, no," Lucy insisted. "It's perfect. It doesn't need any more salt."

"Pepper?"

"More pepper would have spoiled it," Estrella said. "Your stew doesn't need another thing."

"That's good, then," the peddler said, and the three of them ate until there wasn't a drop of food left in the skillet.

Over dinner they talked. Patrick drew out of them the sad story of the losses they had suffered, both women all the while fending off tears. When he learned that Carlos had joined Sam Houston's army, Patrick realized that their trials were not yet over. "You are two brave ladies, that's for sure," he told them. "And I mean to take right good care of you now that the good Lord has delivered you and your beefsteak into my hands." The Irishman's blue eyes twinkled beneath the starlight. "Now, to start with, I'm going to make us a nice pot of strong tea."

"Tea?" Estrella and Lucy chorused. "You mean coffee."

Patrick shook his head. "Tea. It's a drink that soothes you. No, tea is what we need to give us all a good night's sleep so that we'll be fresh for our travels in the morning."

And even though Lucy and Estrella looked warily at

the cups of tea he prepared for them, they drank the beverage and did feel drowsy and relaxed after they had finished.

Lucy slept that night. It was the first night in many that she had been able to sleep the whole night through. Maybe it was the tea, she thought the next morning, or maybe it was the presence of Patrick James O'Houlihan—something had given her a measure of hope.

Chapter 11

⁘═══⁘

THE NEXT MORNING THEY CROSSED THE BRAZOS River with the peddler's help. He had gone exploring before Lucy and Estrella awoke, and he had found a shallow part of the river where it was easier to cross. He insisted that Lucy and her mother sit on the wagon seat together while he waded across, leading the horses. After that he went back for his own small wagon with one horse, and, while Lucy and Estrella watched, he crossed safely once again.

"Where to now, ladies?" he asked after he had changed into dry clothes, which included another checked jacket. "I'm a lost man in this territory."

Washington-on-the-Brazos," Lucy said. "That's where Sam Houston is supposed to be. We'll be safe there."

"Safe," Patrick O'Houlihan said. "I like the sound

of that. You go ahead, and I'll follow close behind."

Lucy clicked to the horses, slapped the reins across their backs, and, with Blanca trailing from a rein attached to the wagon, they started on what she hoped would be the last part of their journey to safety.

It took the better part of the day, but finally, by late afternoon, they could see a clump of buildings in the distance, the buildings of the small town of Washington-on-the-Brazos. "That's it," Lucy called back excitedly to Patrick. "We're almost there!"

He smiled and waved as the two wagons moved forward.

As they got closer, Lucy could see that there were quite a few wagons camped outside the town. Estrella saw them, too, and she asked, "Why are they there? I don't understand it. Why aren't all those people staying in town?"

"Probably too many folks for the town to handle," Lucy said. "I guess everybody had the same idea we did—come to Washington-on-the-Brazos and be safe with Sam Houston."

But when they finally reached the edge of the town they learned that they were still far from safe—and they were given this news by none other than the Shumanns!

Angry, close to fury, the Shumanns had recognized the Bonner wagon from a distance when they saw Blanca trotting behind.

Dirk waited until Lucy drew close, and then he hailed her. "Lucy, stop! Wait, we're over here." The sound of Dirk Shumann's voice was an unwelcome surprise for Lucy.

"Estrella, is that you? Estrella!" Greta Shumann shouted as she ran from their wagon's campsite to where Estrella Bonner sat on the wagon seat.

"Lucy, stop the wagon," her mother ordered. After Lucy reined the horses to a halt, Estrella slipped down from the wagon seat. "Greta, what is it?"

"Oh, Estrella." Greta Shumann burst into tears as Estrella Bonner patted her shoulder. "I'm so glad to see someone I know. It's been terrible, just terrible. We've lost everything!"

I don't understand," Lucy said to Dirk. "What happened?"

Johann Shumann appeared. "What happened?" he said. "I'll tell you what happened! Those Mexicans—"

"They didn't care that we were neutral," Dirk interrupted.

"They didn't care about anything," Greta said.

"Let me tell it," Johann Shumann roared.

It took a few minutes for the Shumanns to calm down enough to tell the Bonners their story. Just after they had been warned to leave, one part of the Mexican Army had marched in the direction of their ranch. The Shumanns had greeted them, offered them food, and explained that they were neutral.

"We told them we were farmers and ranchers," Johann Shumann said. "We explained that we were on no special side, that we just wanted to be allowed to live in peace—"

"Peace!" Greta Shumann interrupted bitterly. "What do such men know of peace?"

"Greta," Johann Shumann barked angrily at his wife. "I'm talking!"

He went on telling Estrella and Lucy the rest. It seemed that the Mexicans didn't recognize the Shumanns' neutrality. They sacked the house and gave the Shumanns ten minutes to get out with whatever they could carry.

The three Shumanns had run back and forth from the house to the one wagon that the Mexicans let them keep. They made as many trips as they could in that short space of time, carrying clothes, blankets, pots—any belongings they could grab.

"My beautiful dishes that my mother had brought from the old country," Greta Shumann wept in Estrella Bonner's arms. "And my silver, and the crystal glasses of my grandmother—all gone!"

"Dishes and glasses," Johann Shumann said angrily. "Who cares about such nonsense? But our ranch, our house—"

"What happened to your house?" Estrella asked, suddenly pale.

"They burned it," Dirk said. "After we took our few belongings, they burned the house down to the ground."

"Oh, Lucy," Estrella said, looking up at her daughter, who still sat on the wagon seat. "Our beautiful *hacienda*—it's gone."

"What do you mean?" Johann Shumann asked.

"Your house isn't gone! Oh, no, your house still stands. Those stupid Mexicans!"

"What?" Estrella said. "I don't understand."

"They didn't burn your house. They let it stand. Ramiro's boy Paco actually told them that the house belonged to one of the men who died at the Alamo—one of the men who fought against them—and yet they didn't burn your house down."

He saw Estrella and Lucy exchange glances, and he went on. "It's strange, isn't it? That's what I think, too. Here Paco tells them that the house belongs to an enemy—he told us later that's what he said—"

"Paco said that our house belonged to an enemy of Mexico?" Lucy asked in disbelief.

"Well, he said it belonged to someone who died at the Alamo. That's the same thing, isn't it? And then he told them that the women of the family had gone away in a wagon, and after they heard all that they still didn't burn your house down. It's not fair!"

"Would you have felt better if they had burned our house down, too?" Estrella asked icily.

Johann Shumann looked a little shamefaced. "I didn't mean that, Estrella, but still, you would think they'd respect our neutrality. Now we have nothing left."

"You still have your land," Lucy said. "After we win the war, you can go back to it."

"After *we* win the war," Johann Shumann jeered. "What makes you think *we* will win the war? Sam Houston is on the run from Santa Anna."

"You mean Houston and the Texas Volunteer Army aren't in Washington-on-the-Brazos?" Lucy asked.

"They pulled out days ago," Dirk said. "They've been retreating ever since the Alamo."

"That doesn't mean they're on the run," Lucy said loyally. "It probably means they're trying to hunt Santa Anna down. I wonder if they know the direction the Mexican Army is taking?" Lucy asked, remembering all the confusion on the road. "The Mexicans are pretty close behind us. Do you suppose Sam Houston knows that?"

"I don't know and I don't care," Dirk responded. "They didn't do anything to protect us or our ranch. Why should we care about them?"

Lucy looked at him with disgust and said, "Dirk, you—you're—" and finally she blurted out the worst thing she could think to say. "You're no Texan!"

The three Shumanns looked at Lucy as though she had lost her mind, and finally Estrella asked, "But why are you camped out here? Isn't there any place that you can stay in Washington-on-the-Brazos."

"Oh, sure," Johann Shumann said bitterly. "There are hotels and rooming houses and the like, but—"

"They're charging a fortune," Greta Shumann chimed in.

"And we have to save every penny we've got to build another house," Dirk added. "If we ever can lay claim to our land again, that is."

"But meanwhile?" Estrella asked. "You're just going to stay camped out here?"

"We'll manage," Johann Shumann said. "We're not rich, owning a house and all, like some folks."

"Rich!" Estrella said, tears coming to her eyes. "I wouldn't care if my house had burned to the ground if my William was still alive and if I knew that Carlos was safe."

"Will Bonner acted downright irresponsible," Johann Shumann said.

"And Carlos isn't a whole lot better," Dirk chimed in.

"My father and brother are brave men," Lucy said angrily. "They did what they had to do."

"Sure, sure," Dirk jeered. "And what have you got to show for all their bravery? Two women, traveling alone, no one to take care of them—"

"Well, now, I wouldn't say that exactly, sonny." Lucy had forgotten Patrick James O'Houlihan, but now he appeared like a small Irish leprechaun to stand by her side. "These ladies have someone to take care of them, and that someone is myself—Patrick James O'Houlihan, at your service!"

Dirk stared open-mouthed at the short, round man in the brightly checked jacket. "Who's this?" he asked Lucy.

Before she could answer, Patrick O'Houlihan said, "I think I already told you that, and we can't be standing about here just passing the time of day, either. Miss Lucy, isn't it time we were heading into town to see if we can find a place to lay our heads tonight? I think your ma looks a little bit weary."

"Of course, Patrick, you're right. Come on, Ma."

The two Bonner women swept past the Shumanns and climbed onto the wagon seat once again. Lucy clicked to her horses, looked back to make sure that Blanca was securely tied, and then called to Patrick O'Houlihan. "Patrick?"

"Right behind you, Miss Lucy," he called from his wagon seat. "Coming right along. Don't worry, I'll make sure nothing happens to you ladies."

The Bonners drove past the Shumanns, nodding to their old neighbors as they passed, and headed for the small town of Washington-on-the-Brazos.

Once they arrived, Lucy made inquiries about where she could stable her horses and where she and her mother could stay.

Patrick O'Houlihan explained that he would turn the back of his wagon into a comfortable bed, and that's where he elected to sleep. "But don't you worry, Miss Lucy. After I see you ladies comfortably settled, I'll find a quiet corner for my wagon, probably near the stable where we put the horses, and then I'll be right along to see that you and your ma are all right. The idea! Saying you had no one to take care of you when Patrick James O'Houlihan is nearby!"

Lucy drove to a small rooming house at the edge of town, where they found the cost of a room to be quite reasonable. Lucy helped her mother settle in their room with a few of their belongings which would make Estrella feel more comfortable. Then she drove the wagon to a stable, with Patrick O'Houlihan following close behind.

The stableman listened intently to the orders Lucy gave him about Blanca and her other horses and then asked, "You folks part of the runaway scrape, I guess!"

"Runaway scrape?" Lucy asked, puzzled.

"That's what folks hereabouts call it—people running from the Mexican Army. That what happened to you?"

"That's what happened," Lucy said. "But we didn't know which way to run. We met up with the Mexican Army when we thought they were way south of here."

"The Mexicans this far north?" The stableman looked surprised. "Didn't know that."

"What about Sam Houston and the Texas Volunteer Army?" Lucy asked. "Do you think they know?"

The stableman shrugged. "Sure hope so. Sam Houston's got to stand and fight sometime. Wouldn't like to find Santa Anna on my doorstep tomorrow morning."

Suddenly Lucy felt overwhelmed with worry for her younger brother, and it showed in her face. "Now, don't you worry your pretty head about that," Patrick counseled, realizing instantly what was on her mind. "Why don't you get back to your ma, Miss Lucy? We passed a fine eating establishment back a-ways. Maybe you ladies'll join me there later for a bite of supper?"

The stableman looked at Patrick. "You sure talk funny and fancy. You from back east?"

"I'm from further than that," Patrick said with a smile. "I'm from Ireland!"

"Ireland!" The stableman was impressed. "I never met anybody who came from that far!"

Lucy left the two men and walked down the street to their rooming house. Estrella was stretched out on the room's only bed. Lucy could see that the mattress was full of bumps and lumps, but her mother didn't seem to mind them one bit.

"This is wonderful, Lucy—a bed, imagine. I never thought I'd sleep in a bed again."

Lucy washed up, using a basin and a pitcher of water, and then she stretched out on the bed, too. "Patrick has asked us to have supper with him tonight," she told her mother, but Estrella had already dozed off.

Lucy closed her eyes and tried to get some sleep, but even though she was tired, she just couldn't fall asleep. She kept remembering the words of the Shumanns, and she got angrier and angrier as she thought about them.

Her father was right, Jesse Lee was right, and Carlos—young as he was—was right, too. There were more important things in life than staying home and staying safe. But, oh—and she was glad Estrella was asleep and couldn't see her tears—wouldn't she just give anything, anything in the world, to see her father, to see Jesse Lee, just one more time!

Lucy took a deep breath and choked back her tears. She didn't want to awaken her mother. So many terrible things had happened to them in the few weeks since the Alamo, and she knew Estrella needed all the rest she could get.

But was it worth fighting and dying if after everything they still lost to the Mexicans? That thought plagued Lucy and wouldn't let her rest. If Sam Houston didn't know what direction the Mexican Army was taking, the Texans could well lose, and that would mean that her father and Jesse Lee and all the others had died for nothing.

Lucy lay still on the bed, her eyes tightly shut, her fists clenched by her sides. That idea was more than she could bear!

Chapter 12

THAT EVENING, LUCY AND ESTRELLA MET PATRICK O'Houlihan in the fine eating establishment he had spoken about, a small restaurant on the main street of the town.

Looking about, Lucy saw that most of the other patrons were women, children, and a few old men. "Looks like everyone's gone off to fight with Sam Houston," Patrick said.

"That's right," a tired waitress who had overheard him said. "Just about anybody who can sit a horse or tote a gun has joined the Texas Volunteer Army."

The waitress recited the day's menu to them. "We've got beefsteak, and somebody shot a couple deer so we got vension steak. There's rabbit stew— tastes kinda strong if you ask me—and there's beans."

The three agreed that beefsteak and beans sounded best, and Lucy added, "Coffee, please."

"Oh, yes, hot coffee," Estrella sighed. "How wonderful it will taste in a proper cup instead of a tin mug."

"And tea, if you please," Patrick O'Houlihan said. "A nice pot of hot tea."

The waitress looked at him. "We haven't got any tea," she told him.

It was clear that Patrick had heard this before, because he didn't look one bit upset by the news. "Just a pot of hot water, then, if you'll be so kind. I'll make my own." He produced a small tin from his jacket pocket.

The coffee came first, and Lucy and her mother drank two full cups before the waitress placed plates covered with large slabs of beefsteak before them.

The three cut into the meat and tasted it, and then Estrella said, "I think the *barbacoa* Patrick made for us was a lot tastier than this."

Lucy agreed. Patrick beamed and insisted on preparing cups of tea for everyone. Lucy only half listened as Estrella and Patrick argued in a friendly way about which was better, tea or coffee.

Lucy looked around the dining room again and saw that other people had come in for supper. But it was still the same—the room was filled as before with women, children, and a few old men. Clearly, Sam Houston's army had gone off somewhere looking for Santa Anna when all along the Mexicans were right behind them. Suddenly she knew what she had to do, and once she had made up her mind she went back to eating her steak with an appetite. Lucy even drank a cup of Patrick's tea and pronounced it delicious.

Estrella looked at her daughter, trying to fathom what was going on in her mind, while Patrick poured more tea.

Early the next morning, Estrella watched from bed as Lucy put on her riding clothes. "I knew it," she said as she watched Lucy dress. "I just knew it."

"Ma—"

"You're going out to find Sam Houston."

Lucy looked at her mother. "You'll be all right, Ma. I'm glad we met up with Patrick O'Houlihan. He'll be company for you until I get back."

"Oh, Lucy," Estrella said wearily. "It's not company I need, it's my family—my husband, my son, my daughter—"

"But, Ma, don't you see?" Lucy pleaded. "If Sam Houston doesn't know where the Mexican Army is coming from, Texas could lose the war. And Pa and Jesse Lee—what did they die for if we lose? They died for nothing."

"Don't say that, Lucy," Estrella said. "I can't bear that idea."

"Neither can I, Ma," Lucy answered. "That's why I've got to get to Sam Houston."

"If anything happens to you, Lucy," her mother whispered, "I'll die."

"Nothing will happen to me, Ma. I promise."

"Your pa promised me, too," Estrella said. "And I'm sure Jesse Lee made a promise just like that."

Lucy was silent, and then she said, "I really think I'm doing the right thing, Ma. Please don't try to make me stay."

Estrella looked at her daughter, dressed in her Mexican riding outfit, her hair pulled back and held with a white ribbon, her black hat in her hand. "All right, Lucy," she sighed. "Go on, now. I'll be here when you get back."

Lucy kissed her mother and walked swiftly out of the room. The heels of her black riding boots clicked a fast rhythm as she ran down the stairs, and Estrella moved to the window of the small room to watch her daughter stride down the street.

Lucy talked to the stableman while she saddled Blanca. Many of the horses of the Texas Army had been stabled with him, and he was able to give Lucy some idea of the direction Sam Houston had taken when he had left Washington-on-the-Brazos.

Before she rode out of town, Lucy stopped to see Patrick O'Houlihan. "I know it's a lot to ask of you," she said after she had explained her mission. "But if you could keep an eye on my mother—"

"Whoosh, that's nothing at all," he exclaimed. "But I was thinking that I should ride along with you, Miss Lucy. Seems to me you're the one who needs a watchful eye."

"I'll be all right," Lucy said, smiling. "You'd be

surprised at how well I can take care of myself. When I come back I'll tell you about my ride to the Alamo, and about the time I met General Santa Anna."

Patrick O'Houlihan shook his head. "You do get around for someone so young," he told her. "If you don't mind my asking, how old are you, Miss Lucy?"

"Almost seventeen," Lucy said. "But I don't think that matters. Somehow I feel a lot older."

"You certainly act a lot older," he said. "It's the war, I guess. You go on, Miss Lucy, if you're sure you got to. I'll look after Miss Estrella."

"I'm sure I've got to," Lucy said. She mounted Blanca and turned to give Patrick a final wave.

"Sam took the road to Liberty," the stableman had told Lucy, and with no real knowledge of the territory before her, she followed the road the man had pointed out, the road that led to the town of Liberty.

Lucy remembered how she had felt when she rode to the Alamo. At the time, she knew she was doing a dangerous thing, but she had still enjoyed the feeling of freedom that riding Blanca gave her.

When she rode to the Alamo it was to bring Carlos back, but she had also been riding to see Jesse Lee Powell. There would be no Jesse Lee for her this time, and she just hoped that there would be no troop of Mexican soldiers, either.

It was the beginning of April, and as the sun rose higher Lucy began to feel warm, too warm. Her mother wouldn't have been happy to see her do so, but

Lucy pushed her hat off her head, and it bobbed against her back, saved from falling by the chin ribbon that now rested against her throat.

The road ahead was clear, and Lucy leaned forward in her saddle to urge Blanca on. The road curved, and still there was nothing—nothing that she could see. Suddenly Blanca stumbled in her headlong gallop, and before Lucy understood fully what was happening, she felt herself flying out of the saddle and over Blanca's head onto the dirt road. She didn't feel scared, only bewildered, and then she felt nothing at all.

Lucy didn't know how long she had been unconscious, but when she came to, she was lying under a tree, and the faces of the people around her wavered, slightly out of focus.

There was someone who knelt beside her and propped her head up against his knee. "Lucy." The person's voice sounded familiar but far away. "Lucy . . ."

She opened and shut her eyes a few times, and the focus became clearer. She looked up into the face of the man holding her, and at the sight of him she tried to sit upright.

"Take it easy, Lucy, take it easy."

She looked again at the familiar face and felt a pang—half sorrow, half happiness. It was Juan Seguin—her good friend and childhood love. But Juan had been at the Alamo, and he was dead. If she could see him so clearly, it meant that she was dead, too. She didn't want to be dead, she knew that much, but at least she was seeing a friend from her living past. Did that mean that she would soon meet up with Pa and Jesse Lee, too?

"Juan," she said, wondering why her ribs hurt so much when she tried to find the breath to speak. "Juan, is Pa with you?"

Juan shook his head, and Lucy heard one of the other men say, "Did you say that's Will Bonner's daughter? She must've hit her head harder'n we thought. She's forgotten that her Pa is dead."

Lucy tried to explain—she hadn't forgotten anything—but weren't they all dead together? She tried to ask that question, but she was so tired that she had terrible trouble saying the words. "Juan," was as far as she got. "Juan," she said, and then her eyes shut once again.

"Easy, Lucy," she heard Juan say. "You'll be all right, just take it easy. Don't try to rush things."

She drifted off again, and when she came to the second time her mind was much clearer. She realized that the pain she felt in her ribs and along the side of her head was far too real to belong to a dead person.

But if she was alive, then who had been telling her to take it easy? In her dreamlike state she had thought it was Juan Seguin, but it clearly couldn't have been Juan. She was alive, all right, her aching head told her that, but Juan was dead.

"Lucy." She heard that familiar voice once again, and then someone kneeling beside her said, "Lucy, are you feeling better?"

She opened her eyes as wide as she possibly could. She hadn't been dreaming after all. There he was— Juan Seguin! "Juan." Lucy forced herself to sit up, though every movement increased the hammering in her head. "Juan, it *is* you!"

Juan smiled, his smile erasing some of the lines of fatigue in his face. "I guess you are better, Lucy. For a while there, we thought—"

Lucy sat bolt upright. She didn't care about her throbbing head. She threw her arms around him. "Juan," she said. "It really is you—you're alive!"

"Lucy, *mi novia*." Juan's voice was sweet, not teasing at all. "Of course I'm alive. What did you think?"

Lucy let go of him only so she could get a better look. "But you were at the Alamo! We heard that everyone who was at the Alamo was dead. But you're alive, Juan, alive! I'm so happy."

Now it was Juan's turn to hug her to him. "Lucy, you are my *novia*, after all—my sweetheart. Only a *novia* could care that much about a man."

Lucy didn't pay any attention to Juan's talk of *novias* and sweethearts. She needed to understand what had happened to the men of the Alamo. "But how, Juan?" she asked. "How did it happen? We heard that all the men at the Alamo were killed."

"They were," Juan said bitterly. "General Santa Anna and his red flag of death—he meant it. No man was left alive in the Alamo, Lucy. I'm sorry."

"But you—"

"I wasn't in the Alamo," Juan explained. "Colonel Travis had sent me out on a mission. I went to Goliad. Travis was still hoping that General Fannin could spare him some men, but Fannin had his own battles to fight, and he couldn't do it."

"Was there anyone else?" Lucy asked hoarsely. "Had Colonel Travis sent anyone else out on a mission? Anyone at all, Juan?"

Juan shook his head. "I don't know, Lucy. I wish I did. I just know what happened to me. By the time I left Goliad, the Alamo had been captured. There was nothing for me to do but to join up with Sam Houston. I'm sorry, Lucy. I wish I could give you more news about your father."

"Pa, of course," Lucy said, and she didn't explain to Juan that it wasn't just her father she was thinking about.

"But Lucy," Juan asked. "What are you doing out here, riding by yourself?"

Lucy explained that she and her mother had left their ranch on the advice of Sam Houston's couriers, and she told Juan how disappointed they were to discover that Sam Houston and his men had left Washington-on-the-Brazos when they had arrived there.

"We ran into Mexican soldiers just on the other side of the Brazos," Lucy told him. "And I wasn't sure if Sam Houston knew the direction the Mexican Army was taking, so I thought I'd better ride out and find him."

Juan shook his head. "Just like that? You decided to ride out to find our army in the middle of a war?"

"There wasn't anyone to send," Lucy explained defensively. "There are no men left in town, leastways nobody fit to ride."

"My Lucy," Juan said, looking at her with admiration. "I never imagined that my quiet Lucy would grow up and become a heroine."

"I'm no heroine," Lucy protested. "Not like the men who died at the Alamo."

"Good men died at the Alamo," Juan said. "But the rest of us have to go on, Lucy, and after we win this war, those of us who are left will have to make a life with each other."

It was a pleasure to hear someone talk about Texas winning the war, Lucy thought, especially when she remembered the Shumanns and the way they had acted. It was so good to find Juan alive—an old friend from a happier time in her life—that she couldn't help herself. She just had to throw her arms about Juan and give him another hug. "Juan, you just don't know what it means to me to see you again—it's wonderful!"

Juan's answering hug was not the brief embrace of an old friend. He responded by gathering her close to him and tightly holding onto her. "And you don't know what it means to me, Lucy, my love," he answered, his voice husky with emotion. "This war—so many of our friends dead, so many homes destroyed. But seeing you, I know there's something worth fighting for, something worth living for. Because when this war is all over, Lucy, *mi novia . . .*" He hesitated and then said it once again, and this time *mi novia* was not the playful joke of a grown man speaking to a little girl. "*Mi novia,*" Juan breathed. He tilted her face up ever so gently, and his mouth was light and sweet on hers.

For a few minutes Lucy stayed nestled in his arms. It felt so good to be held by this man, her childhood friend who clearly wanted to be more to her than a friend. *Novia* was what a man said when he spoke of the girl he planned to marry.

And why not? She was no longer ten years old to his twenty. Now she was sixteen—almost seventeen—and he was twenty-six. They were both the right age to be married.

Jesse Lee, she thought. But Jesse Lee was dead, and so was her father. She didn't know if Carlos was dead or alive, and it was so wonderful to have a man in her life once again, a loving man who would take care of her and her mother.

For a minute Lucy felt as though she had a future to look forward to again. She would marry Juan and everything would be all right. But then she realized that she was trying to bring an old dream back to life, a dream that had died when she met Jesse Lee. When she was a little girl she had thought she was in love with Juan, but after she met Jesse Lee she understood the real meaning of love, and she knew that what she felt for Juan was warm affection, nothing more than that.

But perhaps that was all she would ever have in her

life now that Jesse Lee was dead. Couldn't she make do? Wouldn't she be wise to compromise and stop yearning for her lost love?

"No," Lucy said out loud. "No!" She moved out of the comforting circle of Juan's arms. "No, Juan, I'm sorry."

Juan didn't understand. Lucy had always cared for him. Didn't she care for him now?

Lucy felt that she owed Juan an explanation. "There was someone else at the Alamo, Juan," she said. Then she stopped trying hard to find the words.

"There were many good men at the Alamo," Juan said, and he waited for her to go on.

"But there was one—someone very special"—Lucy's voice broke—"someone I loved . . ."

Juan took a step back from Lucy. "Of course," he said. "I remember. It was one of the men from Tennessee, wasn't it?"

Lucy nodded. "Yes. Jesse Lee Powell, that was his name." She was happy to say his name out loud. "Jesse Lee Powell," she repeated. "Jesse Lee."

The name seemed to echo all around them. If only she could hear him answering to his name, but that could never happen again. She and Juan were alone, facing each other near a dusty Texas road.

"I'm sorry, Lucy," Juan said softly, "so sorry that this should have happened to you."

"I guess it happened to a lot of people," Lucy said, thinking of her mother and her loss. "I'm not alone."

"No, you're not, and . . ." Juan hesitated. "Maybe someday you won't have to be alone, Lucy, if—"

"No, Juan," Lucy said as gently as she could. "I can't. There won't ever be anyone else for me, not ever."

Juan sighed. He had lost her, lost his Lucy, before he could even make her his. But now he had to think of other things. "Do you feel well enough to ride, Lucy?"

Lucy suddenly remembered her mission, and she felt ashamed for having let her personal feelings get in the way. "I do," she said. "But what about Blanca?"

"Blanca's fine," he told her. "We picked a stone out of her hoof. Let's find Sam Houston. I know he'll want to hear what you have to tell him."

Chapter 13

═══════ ◈ ═══════

IT TOOK TWO HOURS OF HARD RIDING BEFORE LUCY, Juan, and the scouting party arrived at Sam Houston's headquarters.

As they passed through the lines of the Texas Volunteer Army, Lucy couldn't help but make comparisons between the two armies. Santa Anna's men were in uniform, well armed, with plenty of cannon and horses. The Texas Volunteer Army was just that—a group of untrained volunteers who had banded together to fight. Some had uniforms; some didn't. Lucy didn't see many cannon, and there was a casual disorder about the men from Texas.

As Juan led her to Sam Houston, Lucy wondered if this group of volunteers had a chance against the highly organized Mexican Army.

There was an air of excitement in Sam Houston's

tent. Houston said briefly, "Knew your father, Miss Bonner," but it was clear that he had other things on his mind. "Look who we have here," he said to Lucy and Juan.

A scouting party from the Texas Army had captured a Mexican courier. Now the man stood in the tent, stiff and formal in his elegant uniform. He was just another soldier as far as Lucy could see, and she didn't understand why Sam Houston and the men around him were so excited.

But then Sam Houston said, "Look at this," and he picked up a worn leather dispatch case that had been taken from the Mexican courier. "Look!"

Lucy gasped when she saw the name that had been etched into the soft leather: *William Barrett Travis.* "That's Colonel Travis's case," Lucy said. "I saw it when I was at the Alamo. Is Colonel Travis here—alive? What about Pa and—"

"Lucy, easy." Juan's hand was on her shoulder.

"I'm sorry, Miss Bonner," Sam Houston said. He was a big man and loomed over Lucy when he spoke. "Colonel Travis isn't alive. Neither is anyone else from the Alamo. This dispatch case is part of the spoils from the Alamo, that's what it is." He turned to the Mexican courier, who was shifting uneasily from one foot to another. "What's your name, soldier?"

The Mexican stood up straight and saluted. "I am Captain Miguel Bachiller, aide to General Santa Anna."

"Aide, huh?" burly Sam Houston said with scorn.

"You belong to some fine army there, Captain Bachiller, when you use things that belong to dead men."

Captain Bachiller looked embarrassed, then nervous as the Texans crowded about him.

"Were you at the Alamo?" someone asked.

"Hey, maybe he killed Travis himself."

"Maybe we ought to give him what he gave Travis and Bowie."

"Leave him alone." Sam Houston's roar was heard above everyone else's voice. "We got bigger catfish to fry."

"I wasn't at the Alamo," Bachiller said nervously in broken English. "Truly I wasn't. I was given the orders in this case. I am a messenger, nothing but a messenger. You can't shoot a messenger."

"I reckon we can shoot whoever we like," one of the Texans drawled, "as long as we got him prisoner."

"I told you never mind about him," Sam Houston shouted again. "Take a look at what he's got in this dispatch case. Can anyone make heads or tails of it?"

The men crowded around to look at a crudely drawn map and a sealed letter of instructions that was quickly opened. "I think Santa Anna sent this man out especially for us to catch him," Sam Houston said. "The map doesn't make any kind of sense. He's trying to fool us into thinking his men are moving north."

"No," Lucy said, forcing herself to be heard over the noise in the tent. "What he says there is true! Santa Anna's men are moving north. I saw them."

"What?" Sam Houston roared. "What did you say,

Miss Bonner? Let me hear you say that again, please. You saw some of Santa Anna's men? When? Where?"

Lucy took a look at the crudely drawn map. She wasn't accustomed to reading maps, but that winding black line reminded her of the river she had so much trouble crossing.

"Is this the Brazos?" she asked.

"Sure looks like it to me," Sam Houston said.

"Well, then," Lucy said, "I saw them here—at this curvy part of the river. That's where they tried to steal Blanca."

"Blanca?" Sam Houston asked.

"My horse."

The Texas commander looked at the map and read the instructions once again. "Then we got to figure these are Santa Anna's real plans. This man was delivering them to a Mexican regiment down the line. Boys, what Miss Bonner told us cinches the deal. I wouldn't have believed these papers by themselves, but now that we know how near Santa Anna is to the Brazos we can make some real surprising plans for him. This is it!" he said, laughing as boisterously as a boy. "Here's where the Texas Volunteer Army stops retreating and stands still to fight!"

"What shall we do with him?" one of them asked about Captain Bachiller.

"Lock him up somewhere," Sam Houston said. "Lock him up good. I wouldn't want this messenger loose to carry any messages back to Santa Anna."

"We haven't got time to bother with the likes of

him," one of Sam Houston's aides said. "Why don't we just shoot him and get it over with?"

Lucy could see that Captain Bachiller was doing his best to remain standing tall.

"Nah," someone else said. "Let's just tell the men outside that we've got the jasper who's carrying Will Travis's case. They'll know what to do with him!"

"I said no," Houston shouted. "I said lock him up. You boys'll get your fill of blood before the day is over, but you don't have to start with a prisoner."

Two of the men hustled Bachiller out of the tent, and one of them said, "Maybe we should fly that red flag, too, like Santa Anna did. Then we wouldn't have to worry about prisoners."

"This is the Texas Army," Houston called after him. "We fly only the Lone Star flag. No red flags for us!"

The Lone Star flag and a flag made out of her white scarf, Lucy thought, remembering the day at the Alamo when Jesse Lee had wanted a second flag. *Jesse Lee.* Juan Seguin was still alive. This man Bachiller was alive. Couriers had a better chance than most soldiers. Wasn't there a possibility that Jesse Lee had been a courier, too? She tried to ask Sam Houston that question, but he waved her away. "I'm sorry, Miss Bonner. You're a brave girl and you've done a great thing for Texas, but I don't have time to chat with you right now."

Chat! Lucy wanted to explain that she wasn't interested in chatting, either. There was just one vital question she wanted to ask: was there a chance, any chance at all, that Jesse Lee Powell might be alive? She knew that her father wouldn't have been a courier, but Jesse Lee Powell might have been sent out of the Alamo before that final battle.

"General," she began again.

"Sorry, Miss Bonner." Sam Houston was brusque. "I've got to make plans. No time to talk about anything else. Seguin, please escort Miss Bonner out of here."

Juan Seguin led Lucy out of the tent. He knew what she had wanted so desperately to ask, and he looked at her with pity. "I'm sorry, Lucy."

Lucy blinked back the tears that were prickling against her eyelids. "That's all right, Juan."

She looked around as the men grouped about, some cleaning guns, others attending to their horses, still others stretched out on the ground with their eyes shut. "Are these all the men in the army?" she asked, again wondering how such a small, disorganized group could possibly beat the well-trained Mexican Army of thousands.

"No," Juan told her. "Some of the men are camped a mile or two down the road." Juan seemed to read her mind. "We're all good fighters, Lucy. And don't forget, we've really got something worth fighting for— our land, our homes—"

"Captain Seguin." Sam Houston's voice boomed from his tent. "Come on in here. You, too, Miss Bonner. Let's look at this map again," he said. "This is where you saw the Mexicans, right, Miss Bonner?"

Lucy took another look at the map. "I—I think so."

"Think so?" Sam Houston roared. "Thinking won't do, Miss Bonner. Did you or didn't you see them there?"

Lucy looked at the map and then up at the commander who towered over her. "Yes," she said. "I did."

"You sure, now?"

"I'm sure."

"Good! Then, according to these plans of Santa Anna's, he's going to be coming up this way," Houston said. He pointed to the map again and stabbed at it with his forefinger. "Because he thinks we're holing up right over here. But we're not going to do any such thing, boys. We're going to march into these woods over there. What are they called? Anybody know?"

"That's Buffalo Bayou," one of Houston's aides supplied.

"Right, Buffalo Bayou, that's where we'll be. And when Santa Anna's men march around this way, we'll start shooting from Buffalo Bayou. Plenty of good cover there. Then we'll make our stand here. This place here." He pointed on the map again.

"The plains of San Jacinto," another aide said.

"San Jacinto. That's it. That's where we're going to say goodbye to those Mexicans for once and for all—at San Jacinto. Get the men ready," he instructed his officers. "It's time to march out."

"Now, Miss Bonner, what are we going to do about you?"

"Me?"

"You sure can't come with us. We got to get you somewhere safe."

"I don't care about being safe," Lucy said.

"Your father died at the Alamo, is that right?" Houston asked.

"Yes."

"You got a brother? Where is he?"

"I—I don't know."

"And your mother?"

"Ma's back in Washington-on-the-Brazos."

"Well, I don't want to be the one to face your mother after all this is over and tell her that she lost another of her kin because of me. You wouldn't want me to have to do that, would you, Miss Bonner?"

Lucy shook her head. "I guess not."

"Fine! Then what you got to do is get on that horse of yours—Blanca you said her name was?—and ride out of here. Liberty—you got to get to the town of Liberty. That make sense to you? What about you, Seguin, what do you say?"

"It makes sense to me, General," Juan Seguin said.

"Fine! Then you escort Miss Bonner part of the way. Show her the right road. You can catch up with us at Buffalo Bayou."

Lucy was hustled out of Sam Houston's tent, and she and Juan moved at a run to where their horses were tethered.

As they rode out of the camp, Lucy heard officers giving men orders. Suddenly there was no one stretched out on the ground. Men were running, saddling horses, marshaling themselves into some kind of order.

"Juan." Lucy had trouble speaking as she and Juan galloped down the road. "I just want to say—to thank you—"

"Nothing to thank me for," he told her. "You'll always be *mi novia*. That's how I'll always think of you, Lucy."

They had arrived at a crossroads and reined their horses to a halt. "You go that way, Lucy." Juan pointed out the road to her. He wheeled his horse about. "Take care, *mi novia*—"

"Juan," Lucy called after him. "You take care!" She wasn't sure if he heard her, but then she realized that he must have. She saw him turn halfway in his saddle and raise his hat to her in a final salute.

She watched until she couldn't see him any longer, and then she turned Blanca's head toward Liberty. Saying goodbye to Juan reminded her again of all the other goodbyes she had said over the past few weeks.

As Lucy rode toward Liberty she thought again about the awful tragedies of the Alamo. She could hardly believe it, but the Alamo had fallen only six short weeks ago. Here it was, April twenty-first, and she had lived through years of pain in what had been only a brief month and a half.

Chapter 14

WHEN LUCY RODE INTO THE TOWN OF LIBERTY, SHE was immediately surrounded by curious people who ran out from stores and houses to greet her.

"Where you coming from?" someone asked.

"Have you seen Houston and the army?"

"Do you think we have to pack up and start moving again?" a woman with a baby in her arms asked.

Lucy tried to answer all the questions, but with everyone talking at once no one could hear her answers.

"Give the young lady a little breathing space." A heavy-set man in shirtsleeves wearing a white apron shouldered his way through the crowd. "This way, miss, this way."

He led Blanca to a hitching post in front of a store that bore the sign "General Store—Josiah Calhoun,

Prop.," and after Lucy dismounted she followed him inside.

"Now, Miss—Miss—"

"I'm Lucy Bonner, from San Antonio."

"San Antonio," someone said. "Did you have anyone at the Alamo?"

"My father," Lucy said, "and—and—"

Josiah Calhoun, proprietor of the store, saw that Lucy had trouble going on. He whisked away a large red cat from the top of a cracker barrel and dusted the top of the barrel with the edge of his apron. "Here, Miss Bonner, you look as though you've ridden a ways. You sit right down here now."

Lucy perched on top of the barrel, and as the people of Liberty crowded around her she told them about Sam Houston and his plans to meet General Santa Anna in battle.

"Well, now, it's about time, isn't it?" a gray-haired man commented. "Glad to see Houston's finally stopped running. Thought for a while that Santa Anna was going to chase him clear out to California and into the Pacific Ocean."

"You think you could do better?" another man asked. "How come you're not with the volunteers if you think you can do better?"

"I'm too old," the man mumbled unhappily. "That's the only thing that's stopping me. I'm too old."

Lucy looked about her. The scene reminded her of Washington-on-the-Brazos. There were no young men

158

about, just women, children, and men too old to fight.

"I just want to stop running," the woman with the baby said. "We've been running like hens being chased by a fox. First this way, then the other—a body doesn't know where to turn."

Lucy took a deep breath. "I don't think we're going to have to run anymore. I think this is it—leastways, that's what Sam Houston said. He said San Jacinto is where the Texas Volunteer Army is going to make its stand."

"San Jacinto—that's right nearby."

"Only a hoot and a holler down the road."

"If there's fighting, we'll hear the guns."

"And if Houston loses, this is the first place them Mexicans are going to come to."

"We're not going to lose," Lucy said shortly. "We can't."

"Oh no?" someone said to her. "I bet that's what they thought at the Alamo, too."

Lucy looked at all the people clustered around her, some of them very frightened, and she wished she was at San Jacinto with the army. It was easier to fight, she decided, than to wait in the background to hear the news. She stood up. "I have to take care of my horse," she said. "Is there a stable nearby?"

"Right in back of my store," Josiah Calhoun said, taking off his apron. "Come on, Miss Bonner, I'll give you a hand."

Lucy walked her horse around back to the stable,

and she removed Blanca's saddle while Josiah Calhoun prepared to rub the animal down.

It was while they were taking care of Blanca that they heard it, the noise that had reminded Lucy of thunder when she and her brother Carlos had ridden away from the Alamo.

Lucy had thought of thunder then, but now it reminded her of nothing but what it was—the sound of cannon and guns, the sound of danger and death.

"It's started," Josiah Calhoun said.

"I know," Lucy said, leaning against Blanca. "I know."

How many will die this time? she wondered. How many people I care about will I lose this time? Carlos—she hadn't had much time to think about Carlos—and she had a terrible feeling that he was out there somewhere, in the thick of the battle. And Juan was certainly fighting beside Sam Houston.

When they had ridden away from Sam Houston's camp, Juan had tried to comfort her with the thought that this time the Texas Volunteer Army had a much larger force than the one that had faced Santa Anna at the Alamo. "We only had around a hundred and eighty men at the Alamo, but now we have over eight hundred," Juan had said proudly.

But Lucy, remembering the Mexican Army, thought, *Our eight hundred men against their thousands.*

She didn't say anything, but Juan seemed to know

what she was thinking, and he laughed, pretending to be the old, carefree Juan. "And don't forget," he said. "They're mostly all Texans!"

Lucy had done her best to smile when he said that, but now, as she stood beside Josiah Calhoun, staring down the empty road to San Jacinto, she felt as though she would never be able to smile or laugh again.

"I wonder when we'll know something," she said.

"When the guns are quiet," the storekeeper answered. "Then we'll know."

Lucy decided that this April twenty-first was the longest day of her life. The afternoon went on endlessly, the hours punctuated only by the sound of guns. Then it was early evening, and the sky was bright with a fiery sunset. Twilight came, and the guns still echoed. A few stars poked their way through the evening sky, and the sound of guns could still be heard. Then it was dark, and with the dark came silence—an awful, frightening silence.

People crept out of their homes and gathered in front of the general store. They had a need to be together, a hope that they could find some comfort as they looked around at familiar faces. They stood quietly on the dirt street and waited—but for what? They peered out through the darkness at the road that led from Liberty to San Jacinto, but they saw nothing and no one.

Who would come riding down the road—the Texas Volunteer Army or the victorious Mexicans? They didn't know, but they all feared that the Texans had lost again. And this time the loss would be even more terrible than the one they had suffered at the Alamo, because there were more lives at stake.

Josiah Calhoun was the first one to break the silence. "Seems to me that it was over too quick," he said.

"Too quick?" Lucy asked. She couldn't believe him. To her, the day had been endless.

"You don't understand, Miss Bonner. A big battle like that—with our side so outnumbered—maybe it didn't take any time at all for the Mexicans to whip our boys. May seem like a long time to you, but it's only been a few hours."

"Yup," an old man agreed sadly. "'Fraid Josiah's right. A holding action is the best we coulda hoped for, and it doesn't seem to me that our side held them off for long enough."

Lucy looked at the people around her—the people who had already given up hope—and she felt a surge of impatience. "Well, I can't believe that we lost," she said. "None of us really knows what happened, but I tell you, I'm sure going to find out!"

"What are you going to do?" Josiah Calhoun asked.

"I'm going to ride to San Jacinto and find out what happened, that's what I'm going to do! I'm going to saddle Blanca."

"You can't do that," the woman with the baby said. "It wouldn't be safe."

"The idea!" someone else said. "A young girl riding

out in the dark all by herself. You don't know who you're liable to meet up with!"

Lucy realized that just six short weeks ago she would have agreed with these people; she would have waited quietly with the rest of them. But that was the old Lucy—the Lucy before the Alamo, the Lucy before Jesse Lee, the Lucy who hadn't faced up to the Mexican Army twice. That Lucy was gone forever. This Lucy—the new Lucy she had become—knew that she'd rather ride out in the darkness by herself than wait with this huddle of people, not knowing what had happened.

She couldn't explain how she felt, and she didn't feel that she had to. She just had to go, to ride to the plains of San Jacinto and find out what happened. But there was still something of the old Lucy left in her, the polite Lucy who had been brought up not to sass folks, especially older folks. "I sure want to thank you for your concern," that Lucy said. "And I appreciate it. But I've just got to ride out there. It's better than standing here, wondering and waiting and worrying—at least for me it is."

Lucy lit a spark in some of the people standing on that dusty street.

"She's right," Josiah Calhoun said, whipping off his apron. "I'm going with Miss Bonner. Anyone else want to come along? You're welcome."

Finally, Lucy and three men rode out of Liberty. The huddle of people, moving as one body, walked behind them to the edge of town and then stood looking after the four riders as they disappeared down the dark road that led to San Jacinto.

They had ridden way past town when they heard the sound of horses' hooves coming toward them.

"Riders," Josiah Calhoun said, and then a minute later he changed that to, "One rider—and coming fast."

Lucy didn't say anything, but the thought of that one lone rider frightened her. Just *one* rider didn't sound good. If the Texans had won, wouldn't they have sent a whole troop with the good news? One rider, one messenger, maybe one of the few men left, bringing news of defeat. Why else would it be just one rider?

Lucy and the men with her spurred their horses on. If it was bad news, they might as well learn about it quick and get it over with. And if it was good news, by some miracle, well, the sooner they heard it the better.

The four from Liberty saw the man riding toward them by the light of a bright April moon. He saw them, too, and took off his wide-brimmed hat and waved it wildly. Then he started yelling and shouting. At first they couldn't hear him clearly, but soon they were able to make out his words. "Remember the Alamo!" the man was shouting. "Remember the Alamo!"

I'll always remember the Alamo, Lucy thought sadly. *Is he about to tell us that San Jacinto was another battle of the Alamo? Have we lost again?*

The man stood up in his stirrups, and this time they

heard him. "Remember the Alamo! We've won! We've won!"

Lucy spurred Blanca on and passed the other three riders. She was the first one to reach the messenger, and she was so excited that she reined Blanca to an abrupt halt. Blanca reared slightly, pawing the air. The man from San Jacinto also had a few seconds of trouble with his mount, but finally both he and Lucy calmed their horses and faced each other.

"You said—" Lucy gasped, finding it hard to breathe. "Did I hear you say—"

The man grinned, and Lucy thought this was the most beautiful grin on the most beautiful man she had ever seen—he had carrot-red hair, freckles, and missing teeth, but he was beautiful. "Yes, ma'am, the man said. "You heard it right! We won—the Texas Volunteer Army whipped that whole big Mexican Army. Eight hundred of us, and we beat them. We beat them!"

By that time the men from Liberty had reined up beside Lucy, and they asked the same questions that Lucy had tried to ask.

"Did you say we won?"

"We won!" the man whooped. "We sure did win! We got even—made up for what happened at the Alamo, we did. That's how we went in. Did you hear me? Remember the Alamo! That's what everyone was yelling. Remember the Alamo! And we remembered. We sure did—we remembered the Alamo and got our revenge, too."

Lucy started to cry, and the messenger tried to comfort her. "No need for tears, little lady," he said. "Everything's all right now. We won. Texas is ours."

The other men believed that Lucy's tears were those of relief and joy at the news, but Lucy had many other feelings as well. There was no way that this victory could make up for all her losses. Her father was gone, Jesse Lee was gone, and nothing could bring them back, not even victory. But still, she dried her eyes with the back of her hand. They had won, and that meant that she, her mother, and Carlos could go back to their ranch, could try to lead some kind of normal life again.

Carlos—where was Carlos? So much had happened in such a short time, but now the war was over, and she had to find out what had happened to Carlos.

She turned to the men who had ridden out with her from Liberty. "I'm going to San Jacinto," she said. "My brother might be there, and I want to see if my friend Juan Seguin is all right."

"You could wait till morning," Josiah Calhoun suggested.

"I can't wait," Lucy said. "I'm going now."

The messenger said, "If you three fellers'll spread the word, I'll ride back to San Jacinto with this little lady."

"Be happy to do that," Josiah Calhoun said with a grin. "I'll like telling people some good news for a change."

Chapter 15

═══════ ◈ ═══════

WHEN LUCY ARRIVED AT THE PLAINS OF SAN JA-
cinto, she almost turned Blanca around again and
headed back to Liberty. She saw the plains after the
battle, and not even the dark of the night could hide
the terrible sight.

Neither the Texans nor the Mexicans had had the
time to pick up their dead, and bodies were lying all
about, as were men who were wounded. The men who
hadn't been hurt were carrying the wounded to aid
stations, but most of the wounded were still on the
ground. The few doctors who were there moved
among the wounded, trying to stop the bleeding, doing
their best to treat injuries.

When Lucy rode in on Blanca, a man carrying a
wounded soldier in his arms looked up at her as if he

was seeing some kind of vision. "Who are you?" he asked. "What in tarnation are you doing here?"

I—I've come—" *Why had she come?* "I've come to see if I can find my brother and to see if Juan Seguin is all right."

"Juan's all right. I saw him a little while ago. But come to find your brother! Are you crazy? Do you see what's going on here? How do you suppose you could find anyone in this unholy mess."

"I—I—" Lucy faltered. "I'm sorry. I—I didn't know—"

The man looked at her. "As long as you're here, you may as well do some good. I'm Doctor Lewis. Come with me."

"Where?" Lucy asked. "What can I do?"

"Just follow me," the doctor barked. "And don't ask so many fool questions."

Lucy slipped off Blanca, and, leading her horse by the reins, she followed the doctor to a large tent that had been set up at the edge of the field. She looked around and shuddered. The wounded were lying on blankets on the floor of the tent. There was blood everywhere, and the men needed bandages, water, help—everything.

Doctor Lewis laid the man in his arms down gently and then turned to Lucy. "You're not the kind that faints at the sight of blood, I hope."

Lucy swallowed hard. She did feel close to fainting, but she shook her head and made up her mind that she would stay on her feet no matter what. Her father had died at the Alamo. Jesse Lee had died at the Alamo. They had suffered far more than she would ever know. The least she could do was try to help the wounded. She looked at the doctor. Her face was pale, but she said, "I've never fainted in my life, and I won't faint now."

The doctor nodded grimly. "That's good, because we sure don't have time to take care of fainting young ladies. Now, get the basin, bring over that roll of bandages and those scissors over there, and follow me."

Lucy obeyed him, and they moved from one wounded man to another. She helped him staunch blood and cut lengths of bandage, and she handed him whatever he asked for.

Before she knew it, it was close to morning, and Lucy was exhausted. She glanced at Doctor Lewis and saw her fatigue reflected in his face as well. "Don't cut it that long," the doctor snapped at Lucy when she had handed him a piece of gauze. "Can't you do anything right?"

"I'm sorry," Lucy mumbled, her exhaustion bringing her to the edge of tears. "I'm so sorry."

The doctor finished bandaging the man in silence, and then he stood up. He helped Lucy to her feet from where she had been kneeling beside the soldier's pallet. "I'm sorry," Doctor Lewis said. "Didn't mean to talk to you like that. You've done something wonderful here tonight, more wonderful than you know. I couldn't have helped as many men without you."

He looked at the tired girl before him. Lucy's hair had come loose and was falling about her shoulders. She had taken her jacket off hours before, and her once white shirt was stained with blood.

"You know," Doctor Lewis said, "I don't even know your name."

"It's Lucy," she answered. "Lucy Bonner."

"Will Bonner's daughter? I know Will. Wait till I tell him about his wonderful daughter."

"My father's dead," Lucy interrupted. "He died at the Alamo."

"I'm sorry," Doctor Lewis said. "You said you were looking for someone, but it wasn't Will, was it?"

"I'm looking for my brother, for Carlos."

Doctor Lewis shook his head. "Come with me, girl," he said, leading Lucy out of the tent.

The sun was just coming up. "I can't believe it," Lucy said, blinking.

The doctor stood beside her as they looked out over the field before them. Lucy could see the devastation even more clearly. There were still wounded out there, men who had not yet been cared for—and there were still the dead.

"I don't know, Miss Bonner," Doctor Lewis said. "It's not going to be easy to find anyone here today. Maybe you should go home. Where's your mother?"

"She's waiting for me at Washington-on-the-Brazos."

"Well, maybe you should go back to Washington-on-the-Brazos and wait there. Or go back to your ranch. Your brother will come home—if he can."

"No," Lucy said, shaking her head. "I'm not leaving here without some news of Carlos. I can't go back to my mother and tell her I didn't find him."

"But what if—" and Doctor Lewis didn't finish.

"Then I'd rather know now," Lucy said, understanding his incomplete question. "I'd rather know than wait and wait and wait without ever knowing for sure."

"I understand," Doctor Lewis said. "I understand. But"—and he looked out over the field of the dead, the wounded, and the soldiers sitting in exhausted groups—"I don't know how you can find anyone."

"I have to try," Lucy said. "I'll ask, and I'll look."

"Good luck," Doctor Lewis said. "I wish I could help you, but there's not much I can do."

"I know," Lucy whispered, horrified at what she knew she had to do, horrified that one of the dead or mutilated bodies she saw might be Carlos. "This is something I have to do alone."

She left Doctor Lewis standing in front of the aid tent and walked up to a group of men sitting beneath a cottonwood tree.

"I'm looking for my brother," she said. "Carlos. Carlos Bonner."

The men just shook their heads, too tired to speak. Finally, one of them mumbled, "Don't know any Carlos."

Lucy moved on. "I'm looking for my brother." She kept on questioning groups of men, but all she heard was:

"Sorry."

"Never heard of him."

"Wasn't in our regiment."

"I heard of a Carlos Morales—"

"No. It's Carlos Bonner."

"Sorry. I only know Carlos Morales."

Where are you, Carlos? Lucy thought as she went from group to group. *Where are you?*

At the far end of the field she saw a large tent with officers hurrying in and out of it. That had to be Sam Houston's command post. Hopefully, she thought she might find Juan Seguin there, and maybe he could help her find Carlos.

Lucy edged around the center of the field. There was less activity among the trees that ringed the plain than in the center, where many wounded men were still waiting to receive help.

As she rounded a clump of tall pines she heard the sound of laughter. Laughter! She couldn't believe that anyone in this place still had the heart to laugh. Then she saw that the men who were laughing were also passing an earthenware jug from one to the other. They didn't look like Texans, she thought, and as she came closer she saw that they weren't. These men reminded her of Jesse Lee and the other riflemen from Tennessee. Many were dressed in buckskins, a few wore coonskin caps, and all had long-barreled rifles close by.

As she came closer she heard the Tennessee twang when someone said, "Well, now, the thang we got to remember . . ."

Thang. That was just how Jesse Lee pronounced it Lucy thought with a renewed sadness. As she came up to them, one of the men nudged another.

"Well, now," he said. "Look at this pretty little thang."

"Come from Tennessee?" she asked, willing herself not to weep.

"Yes, ma'am," one of the men answered. "Come to take care of these Mexicans for old Davy Crockett's sake."

"Yes," Lucy nodded. "And for Jesse Lee Powell's sake, too."

"Old Jesse Lee? Well, ma'am, we didn't have to do any fighting for old Jesse Lee—reckon he could do it his own self." He shouted back into the tent, "Ain't that right, Jesse Lee?"

A tall, broad-shouldered man stepped out of the tent, a white bandage hiding his forehead and his honey-colored hair. Even though Lucy couldn't see his hair, she could see him—and she could hear him when he asked, "What're you hollering about, Clint? My head's like split in two, anyway. All that hollering isn't doing it one bit of good."

Jesse Lee! It was Jesse Lee!

"I've never fainted in my life, she had said to Doctor Lewis just the night before, but despite what she had said, Lucy Bonner fainted.

When she came to, Lucy was lying on the ground, her head in someone's lap, and she was afraid to open her eyes. She was afraid to open them because she knew that she had only imagined seeing Jesse Lee.

He was dead. He had died at the Alamo. And it was only because she longed for him so much that she had imagined seeing him.

"Lucy girl," she heard someone say. "Lucy, honey, open your eyes."

That voice—it sounded like his voice—but still she was afraid, too afraid to open her eyes . . .

"Lucy, please. Clint, bring some water."

"I don't need any water," Lucy said. "I just need—"

And then, finally, she did open her eyes. "I just need Jesse Lee," she said, sobbing. "I just need Jesse Lee!"

"Darling, darling girl," Jesse Lee said, holding her close to him. "You got him, you got Jesse Lee. It's all right. Everything's all right."

It was minutes more before Lucy could stop crying, and still more minutes before Jesse Lee could convince her that everything really was all right, that he was really alive. *Jesse Lee Powell was alive.*

"Lucy!" Jesse Lee held her against his chest. She

was trembling and telling him that she was sure he had died at the Alamo.

"I guess I would've," Jesse Lee said soberly, "along with all them others, except Colonel Travis sent me first to Gonzales for help and then to Sam Houston. Oh, Lucy, I tried so desperately to find you. I even sent word back with the couriers who were telling you people on the ranches to leave. But they told me you'd already left. No, I wasn't at the Alamo, though maybe I should've been there with Davy and them others—"

"No!" Lucy cried, clinging to him. "No, enough men died there." Suddenly Lucy sat up. "Jesse Lee," she said. "If you're alive, do you think maybe my pa—"

Jesse Lee shook his head. "No, Lucy. He wasn't one of the men Travis sent out of the Alamo. And no man at the fort came out alive."

He saw the tears again forming in her eyes and leaned down to gentle her with a kiss so tender it felt like a butterfly had whisked her lips with its wings. "My Lucy. I didn't know when I'd ever find you again—and now, well, now you've found me."

Lucy nodded. Her pa was gone. But here was Jesse Lee. And maybe Carlos . . . there was still Carlos. What had happened to him? "Jesse Lee," she said, reluctant to move even an inch away from him but knowing that there was still one more thing she had to do. "My brother Carlos—I've got to find out what happened to him."

"Carlos? Oh, you mean Charlie. Lucy, honey, Charlie's just fine. We kept him with us," Jesse Lee said, indicating the other men from Tennessee, "but just a little bit to the rear, when the fighting started. Kept sending him back to get more ammunition and water. You don't think I'd let anything happen to my Lucy's little brother, do you?"

"Jesse Lee," Lucy said, throwing her arms around him once again. "You're wonderful!"

"My beautiful Lucy," Jesse Lee said, hugging her to him. Then he held her away to get a better look at her. "But what are you doing here?" Jesse Lee shook his head. "What are you doing so close to where we were fighting and all. Lucy, you could've been hurt."

"But I'm not hurt—and you're not hurt—and Carlos isn't hurt, Jesse—"

"I know," Jesse Lee said. "But what *are* you doing here, Lucy?" he asked again.

Lucy took a deep breath. Then she said, "It's a long story. It'll probably take me years and years to tell you."

Jesse Lee grinned. "We got years and years, honey. You can tell me your story a little bit at a time, if that's what you want. Just as long as you let me stay real close while you tell it."

Clint came up to them. "You plan on bringing this pretty little thang back with you to Tennessee, Jesse Lee?"

The new woman who was Lucy answered before Jesse Lee had a chance to speak. "No. This pretty little thang is keeping him right here in Texas. He fought for us; he may as well learn to live with us." She looked at Jesse Lee then and smiled. "If it's all right with you, Jesse Lee, I'd like to settle right here."

Jesse Lee and Clint both laughed.

"Pretty *and* pert," Clint said. "I guess you met your match, Jesse Lee."

Jesse Lee looked at her lovingly. "A perfect match—that's what we are all right."

Clint shook his head. "Nobody could ever make me give up on Tennessee," he said.

"And nobody ever will, Clint," Jesse Lee said. "Because only Miss Lucy Bonner could make a man give up Tennessee—and Miss Lucy Bonner is mine. You take Tennessee, Clint. It's all yours."

March 6, 1836
Alamo fell

AFTERWORD
A Historical Note

At the beginning of this story Texas was a territory of Mexico. The Mexican constitution of 1824 had promised statehood to Texas. However, General Antonio López de Santa Anna had violated that portion of the constitution, leaving Texas a territory of Mexico and not a state.

Because of this, the Texans decided that rather than becoming a part of Mexico they would form their own country, the Independent Republic of Texas. It was not Lucy's white scarf with TEXAS written on it that flew above the Alamo along with the Lone Star flag, but one that had the numbers "1824" written on it—to remind the Mexicans of their broken promise.

The defenders of the Alamo held out against the far superior Mexican Army for thirteen days, and, according to the red flag of General Santa Anna, the men

were accorded no mercy when the Alamo fell. During
the battle, the men in the Alamo were aware of Santa
Anna's red flag. They learned of it, and of the strength
of the Mexican Army, from two scouts who, like Lucy
in this story, were allowed to enter the Alamo for that
purpose. Both sides—Mexican and Texan—prided
themselves on not harming women and children,
which is why the women and children who had remained in the Alamo were released when the fighting
was over.

Why didn't Sam Houston send help to the Alamo?
There was so much quarreling and jockeying for posi-
tion in the provisional Texas government that the
danger to the Alamo wasn't recognized until it was too
late. Sam Houston admitted after the war that he had
made a terrible mistake in not sending help to the men
under siege.

After the Alamo fell, the Texan forces commanded
by Sam Houston were in constant retreat until six
weeks later, when Houston and the Texans won a
brilliant victory at San Jacinto, where they went into
battle shouting, "Remember the Alamo!" However,
during those six weeks, many Texans were refugees
and became part of what was known as the Runaway
Scrape.

All wars are cruel, and because, in a certain sense,
this was a civil war—with the Texans trying to secede
from Mexico—it often happened that members of the
same family fought on opposing sides, like the Seguin
family in this story. Today there is a town of Seguin in

Texas, named after the San Antonio family who fought for Texas.

Texas remained an independent republic for almost ten years. In 1845 it became part of the United States of America.

The Mexican point of view regarding Texas in the nineteenth century should be noted. The Mexicans felt that they had allowed people from the United States to settle in their territory—which Texas was—and they expected those people to abide by Mexican laws and rules. They were afraid of losing Texas to the United States and felt that they had every right to put down any insurrection on the part of the Texans.

The Bonners and the Shumanns in this story are fictional, but they are patterned after ranchers who might have lived in Texas during this period. And Jesse Lee Powell, who is also fictional, might have been one of the sharpshooters that "old" Davy Crockett (who was fifty at the time of this story) brought with him from Tennessee when he came to help the Texans in their struggle for independence.

Most of the other characters in this book are factual—Bowie, Crockett, Travis, Houston, Santa Anna, even Captain Miguel Bachiller who was captured carrying Santa Anna's plans in William Barret Travis's dispatch case.

Stephanie Andrews

Is sixteen too young to feel the . . .

Romance, excitement, adventure—this is the combination that makes *Dawn of Love* books so special, that sets them apart from other romances.

Each book in this new series is a page-turning story set against the most tumultuous times in America's past—when the country was as fresh and independent as its daring, young sixteen-year-old heroines.

Dawn of Love is romance at its best, written to capture your interest and imagination, and guaranteed to sweep you into high adventure with love stories you will never forget.

Here is a glimpse of the first six *Dawn of Love* books.

#1 RECKLESS HEART
Dee Austin

The time is 1812, and wild and beautiful Azalee la Fontaine, the sixteen-year-old daughter of a wealthy New Orleans shipowner, is used to getting her own way. There's a war with England going on, and Azalee is warned to curb her reckless ways, but her daring and scandalous behavior makes her a prisoner in more ways than one. While the pirate captain Jean Lafitte can save her from one danger, only Johnny Trent—Azalee's fiery young man in blue—can tame her heart.

Read on . . .

#2 WILD PRAIRIE SKY
Cheri Michaels

The time is the 1840s; the place is the wagon trail west to Oregon. Headstrong Betsy Monroe knows she can meet any danger the trail offers. But Indians, raging rivers, and stampeding buffalo are the least of her worries. There's also Charlie Reynolds, the handsome young trail guide whose irresistible grin means nothing but trouble. When fate throws Betsy and Charlie together only two things can happen: all-out war or a love strong enough to shake the mountains.

#3 SAVAGE SPIRIT
Meg Cameron

The Kentucky frontier of 1780 is a wild place, as Catherine "Cat" Brant finds out when she is captured by Shawnee Indians and carried hundreds of miles from her home. Living in the Indians' village, she falls passionately in love with Blue Quail, a white captive who has been with the Shawnee so long he considers himself one of them. Can Cat make Blue Quail love her enough to leave the Indians and go back to her world?

#4 FEARLESS LOVE
Stephanie Andrews

It is hard to find time for romance during the 1836 Texan War for Independence from Mexico, but fiercely independent sixteen-year-old Lucy Bonner manages to share a few stolen minutes of love with Jesse Lee Powell, a crack young Tennessee rifleman. Lucy risks everything when she tries to save Jesse Lee and the other men of the Alamo and comes face-to-face with the Mexican Army and General Santa Anna himself!

Read on . . .

#5 DEFIANT DREAMS
Cheri Michaels

The War Between the States? Beautiful Savannah McLairn doesn't want to hear about it. This sixteen-year-old southern belle is not going to let the Civil War ruin what she calls her "prime party years." But swept along by the tides of change, Savannah finds herself behind Union lines, very much in danger of losing her rebel heart to a handsome, young Yankee soldier.

#6 PROMISE FOREVER
Dee Austin

Yearning for more love and excitement than she can find in 1840 New Bedford, Massachusetts, Tabitha Walker stows away on a clipper ship sailing for California. Once there, Tabitha finds more excitement than she bargained for. She also finds that she must choose between the two young men who claim her love: Alexi, the Russian aristocrat who can give her the world; and Tom Howard, the American sailor who can only offer himself!

Look for DAWN OF LOVE historical romances at your local bookstore!

First Love from Silhouette

LOOK FOR THESE BOOKS
IN SEPTEMBER

THE PHANTOM SKATEBOARD
Elaine Harper
A Blossom Valley Book!
When Gary Westbrook became a suspect in a bizarre murder, ordinarily cautious Anne risked her life to help him. How could she prove him innocent when all the evidence pointed to his guilt?

ONE IN A MILLION
Kathryn Makris
When a charismatic stranger strolled into the background of a movie Erin was filming, she knew she had found a star. But did this mean outside the movie as well?

A CIVIL WAR
Beverly Sommers
Annie didn't want to spend a whole year in rural West Virginia, especially when it involved seeing her old enemy, Raney. How could she show this lowdown, worthless critter what she *really* thought of him?

FORTUNE'S CHILD
Cheryl Zach
Melissa Abbott was pretty, smart, rich and popular. Tank Robertson, superjock and glamour boy, was crazy about her. Why wasn't she the happiest girl in the world?

America's Favorite Teenage Romance

STILL GOING STRONG!

First Love from Silhouette

BLOSSOM VALLEY BOOKS
by
ELAINE HARPER

plus

in response to those of you who
asked, whatever happened to
Janine and Craig after they
married?

First Love from Silhouette